DO YOU REALLY WANT TO HAUNT ME

A Happily Everlasting Series World Novel

MANDY M. ROTH

Raven Happy Hour, LLC

Blurb

Do You Really Want To Haunt Me: A
Happily Everlasting Series World Novel
(Bewitchingly Ever After)
by
Mandy M. Roth

*Welcome to Hedgewitch Cove, Louisiana, where
there's no such thing as normal.*

Shark-shifter and natural-born hunter,
New York (York) Peugeot, has been living
under a curse placed upon him by his well-
meaning grandmother. She only wanted to
help her grandchildren find their mates, not
drop a spell of chaos upon their heads. The
only way to break the curse is to find his true

mate, but York has no desire to seek out some mythical woman. He's already infatuated with a woman he can't even see and who has a pesky little issue of being living-challenged.

As a ghost, Morgan can't possibly be his mate, or can she? He can't recall a time in his life when he wasn't drawn to her in some form or fashion and when he realizes he's not the only one, he finds himself in a race to save her soul and their future.

Bewitchingly Ever After Series

Don't Stop Bewitching
Everybody Wants to Rune the World
Do You Really Want to Haunt Me
with more to come…

Chapter One

1989

Morgan Dumont rocked in place, her arms high in the air as she mouthed along to the music as one of her favorite bands played on the stage that was nearly within touching distance. The band was performing their encore, playing one of her favorite songs. Not that they had any songs she didn't like.

The concert had been amazing so far. Everything she'd hoped for and more. She'd been a fan of the band for years and owned every single one of their records. The minute she'd learned they'd added a stop in New York City to their tour, she'd attempted to buy herself a ticket, only to find they were sold out.

When a ticket appeared on the kitchen counter as if by magic, with a vase full of flowers and a card wishing her a happy birthday, she'd been surprised her parents had paid enough attention to her likes and dislikes to realize she was a fan of the group, and that they'd even remembered her birthday, as they had forgotten her first twenty.

The parental units weren't known for their listening skills or for being anything close to observant, or warm and affectionate. At least not when it came to her. Her parents had yet to notice the fact she'd cut off most of her hair, leaving her with a cute shag that she teased as high as she could get before dyeing a chunk of the front red. The red, set against her natural black hair, was very noticeable.

But her parents had glanced at her, barely paying any attention, and continued reading their papers at the breakfast table. That had been weeks ago.

They were wrapped up in their own lives. That had always been the way of it.

Her mother was in charge of various social functions, which always seemed to happen at night when Morgan needed sleep or somewhere out of the country. Her father's work kept him away from the house and often out of the country. He often looked at her with something close to disdain in his gaze. Her mother, when home, stayed tucked away in her room, refusing to go out or do anything. She liked to claim that the sun caused wrinkles, therefore she didn't want to be out in it any more than required. On top of that, Muffy spent most of her time in bed, sleeping her days away.

A nanny had raised Morgan. That was probably for the best, considering the only thing her mother seemed to love in life was a small toy poodle that was vicious to anyone who was not Muffy Dumont. Morgan was convinced the canine was the lapdog for Satan himself. Its name was Vapula, and since Morgan had always been fascinated with mythology and theology, and loved to read, she knew darn well that was the name of a demon.

One said to have led legions in hell.

It also seemed to be in a never-ending battle of wills with Morgan's pets. When she was little, she'd wanted pets desperately and, much to her delight, her godfather had gifted her two. A bat and a hedgehog. She loved them both dearly. They tended to fight amongst themselves often, but whenever the dog was introduced into the mix, the bat and hedgehog were suddenly the best of friends. Vapula hated them. And oddly enough, they didn't seem too fond of Vapula either.

Why anyone would name a poodle after a demon was beyond her. Especially someone named Muffy, of all things, but it was what it was.

Her mother's love of the dog knew no limits. It yapped at anyone who got within a three-foot radius of Muffy. She never went anywhere without the small beast. The same could not be said of Morgan.

Her mother went anywhere *and* everywhere without her.

That was fine.

It wasn't as if Morgan craved mother-daughter bonding time with Muffy. In truth, she couldn't recall a time she'd ever wanted such a thing from the woman. The different people who'd cared for her growing up had been kind and nurturing. As were members of the household staff. She could always see the pity in their eyes at the lack of attention her parents paid to her.

The person she was closest to was Millie. She had become a surrogate grandmother of sorts since Morgan had never met her biological grandparents. Technically, Millie was Morgan's nanny, but since Morgan wasn't at an age that she required one, Millie's duties had changed over the years. She now headed the household staff and could almost always be found in the kitchen.

Morgan loved Millie dearly. She also didn't seem too afraid of Morgan's parents whenever they were in one of their famous moods, resulting in tantrums and insults.

Morgan wasn't sure how it was she'd sprung forth from their loins, seeing as how she had virtually nothing in common with them.

For the first few days after finding the concert ticket, she'd been excited, though shocked, at her parents' thoughtful gift.

Typically, they threw expensive items at her and ran the other way, never bothering with silly details like whether Morgan wanted or needed the thing they were giving or if she even liked it. They'd been buying her off since she could remember.

They'd had her to maintain the status quo but they hadn't really wanted a child to cramp their jet-setting lifestyle. Reproducing had been expected of them—a requirement for them to keep their fortune.

There had been an honest-to-the-gods contract with the verbiage requiring them to produce an heir within the first ten years of their marriage, or they'd forfeit their rights to both of their families' fortunes. Mysteriously enough, when Morgan had gotten her hands on the paperwork without her parents' knowledge, she'd found the wording to be odd.

It kept referring to the required child as a sacrifice.

Since both her parents had grown up in the laps of luxury, there was no way either was going to part with the mother lode of paydays, so they'd done what was necessary to fulfill their contractual obligations, even if it meant *sacrificing* by having a child they didn't want.

That was where their parenting had started and ended.

They were shallow and materialistic and clearly had no business raising children.

There were times she wished she'd known what it was like to have a family like the ones on television shows. The kind that all sat around the dinner table together, discussing their day while they ate or played a board game. The type that tucked their children into bed and read them a bedtime story.

Did people like those on the television shows really exist, or were they something Hollywood made up to make the rest of the world feel bad about themselves and want to tune in to get a taste of happiness?

No family she knew in real life was like that.

They were all like hers, parents too rich for their own good, with children left on their own. Though many of the kids

Morgan had grown up around in her social circle had turned out to be crappy adults.

Thankfully, the people who had cared enough about her to raise her in place of her parents had instilled values and morals in her. Something many in her group sorely lacked. Somewhere around the age of sixteen, she'd stopped associating with others in her parents' circle and begun venturing out into the real world and making friends of her own.

True friends.

Not fake ones only in it for the money.

There was only one person in her parents' orbit who Morgan enjoyed spending time around. That was her godfather. His name was Luc Dark, and he seemed to barely tolerate her parents, which only made her like him more.

She'd never been sure of how he'd come to know her parents, or how it had been decided he'd be her godfather. It was easy to see there was an underlying tension between her parents and the man. There were times they came off as not liking one another at all. And Luc was the only person her parents didn't speak down to. They walked on eggshells around him, which was amusing, because he was nothing but a teddy bear to her.

Oddly, the man didn't seem to age.

Neither did her mother, but that was thanks to having a plastic surgeon in her Rolodex.

While Morgan had been on cloud nine after receiving the ticket from her parents, Luc had shown up at the house unexpectedly, looking for her parents, who were in the south of France—*again*. Before he'd left, he'd mentioned something offhand about hoping she enjoyed the show, and she'd known then he'd been behind the gift. That he'd either told her parents what she liked and what to get her for her birthday, or he'd actually gotten her the ticket himself.

He was considerate like that.

As much as Morgan wanted to sing the blues over it all, she couldn't do so in good conscience. So what if her parents didn't really care about her or even remember they had her at times? She had a roof over her head, food on the table, and didn't want for anything. A lot of people weren't that lucky, and she knew it. Knew better than to look the gift horse in the mouth.

But she wasn't above wondering how it was a man as nice as Luc bothered with anyone as shallow as her parental units.

Maybe the man was serving penance for some nefarious act he'd committed in another life. It really was the only explanation to why he'd subject himself to Muffy and Barton Dumont.

Whatever it was, it had left her at the concert of her life and happy.

Music was something she absolutely loved. That and art. The difference was, she was great at art, but couldn't carry a tune with a bucket. That didn't mean she couldn't sing out of tune along with the massive crowd doing the very same thing.

Someone bumped into her, and she twisted to find a man with a tall, spiked mohawk and several nose rings standing there. Since Morgan had a lip ring and an eyebrow ring herself, she wasn't exactly one to judge, but there was something about the man's blue-gray gaze that made unease trickle through her.

She tried to step away and put distance between her and the man, but there was nowhere to go. There were simply too many people at the concert, and it suddenly felt as though they were all crowded up near the stage with her.

The man with the mohawk reached out as if to touch her. The black leather jacket he was wearing had so many silver chains on it that she wasn't sure how the weight of it alone didn't make him topple forward.

A second before his hand would have made contact, another man pushed through the crowd. This one was around six and a half feet tall and looked totally and completely out of place at the concert. He was in a dark gray T-shirt that was snug on him, showing off his rippling, muscular upper body. The jeans he had on didn't have any of the telltale trends like acid washing or man-made holes, but that didn't mean they didn't look awesome on him.

The only thing remotely goth or punk

about him were his black boots. They looked military issue.

The man caught Mohawk Guy's arm and thrust it away from Morgan. The newcomer used his free hand to push his shoulder-length dark hair from his face, showing off his chiseled, angular features. He reminded her of one of the models from fashion magazines who posed for men's cologne ads.

Mohawk Guy boldly attempted to reach for Morgan again, surprising her. It wasn't as if she knew the man, so he had no business trying to touch her at all.

The out-of-place hunk wasn't having any of it. He puffed out his chest and planted himself firmly between Morgan and the man.

"You so much as look at her again and I'll use those chains you're sporting there to beat you to within an inch of your…" His voice, tinged deeply with the South, trailed off as he looked at something toward the back of the arena. He grunted and then growled, "Go. Now."

Mohawk Guy vanished into the crowd

and the cowboy turned slowly to face her, his dark brown gaze locking firmly on her as he did. The temperature around her seemed to flare dramatically.

The band kept playing and the person to her other side danced a bit aggressively and knocked Morgan right into the cowboy. He caught her with ease and additional heat assailed her.

"Hey, darlin'," he said, the timbre of his voice making her breath catch.

Never had she ever imagined herself falling for a country boy, because she was a city girl through and through, but she was literally and figuratively doing just that. He wrapped his powerful arms around her, hugging her.

The moment should have been beyond awkward.

Somehow, it wasn't.

Morgan's arms had a mind of their own as they slid around his waist and returned the embrace, her heart pounding at a level that was nearly as loud as the music.

Country Boy dipped his head, his lips nearing her ear. "I wish I could change it all for you, darlin'. That I could stop it from happenin'. I'm sorry."

She went to her tiptoes and turned her head slightly. "Stop what?"

As she moved her head more, he did the same, and the next thing she knew, their lips were brushing against one another's.

It felt as if a bolt of electricity had gone through her. With a yelp, she grabbed her lower lip and stared at the man, trying to decide if she should be embarrassed by the kiss or tackle him to the floor and kiss him again.

The latter was winning out.

Big time.

He winked and touched her lower lip with the pad of his thumb. "It'll be all right in the end, darlin'. I promise. I've gotta go. I love you."

I love you?

Was the man insane?

Love?

Before she could comment, he backed into the crowd and hurried away. She tried to follow him but found the mass of people pushing in tighter around her. Confused, and hotter than she should be, she stood there, her back to the stage as she touched her lips hesitantly, thinking about the feeling she'd gotten when their lips had connected.

The man had been downright electrifying.

With a shaky laugh, Morgan faced the stage and shook her head at the strange turn the night had taken. What had he meant by wishing he could stop it from happening? Stop what? And what would be all right? Not to mention love. He'd said he loved her. She'd not imagined that or misheard it.

A sinking feeling came over her as she thought harder on it all. Things like that did not happen to her.

Ever.

It had to be an elaborate joke. The man had probably been a fraternity boy who had been put up to a dare by his buddies. They were more than likely having a good laugh at her expense, watching her from a higher vantage point.

That had to be it.

Because there was no reality where a

country hunk like that man and a goth girl from NYC ended up together.

None whatsoever.

The song changed to what she suspected was the last of the night. It was another of her favorites and that helped to drive away some of the sting of being the butt of a joke.

Elation spread through her as she jumped in place, wearing a black mini-skirt, matching thigh-high boots, and a T-shirt that had the sleeves cut off. The shirt proclaimed her love of her home city.

New York.

The song drew to an end, as did the concert.

Still jubilant and on a natural high, Morgan followed the crowd as they exited the arena. There was a lot of shuffling in lines that were three and four people wide, but she managed to make it to the exit. The issue was, it was the wrong exit, on the other side of the arena from near the bus stop.

Life in New York City had left her being one of those people who relied on public transportation or on the driver her parents employed. She'd elected to take the bus to the concert and permit the staff to have time to themselves.

A fast check of her watch let her know she only had a few minutes left before the last bus headed out. She tried to hurry, but the crowd leaving the show was thick and in no rush to disperse or make room for her to get through.

Worried that she'd have to walk home or try to get a cab willing to take her all the way to her parents' home, Morgan turned and went in the opposite direction, remembering seeing a small alleyway that cut behind the arena. It was less than ideal but so was missing the bus.

She was nearly out of breath when she got to it and had to slow to a fast walk.

A stitch started in her side and she touched it, slowing her pace even more. "I have really got to start running again."

There had been a time, before she'd become what her parents liked to refer to as an "angry, antsy young woman," when she'd been into organized sports, gymnastics, martial arts (at her godfather's request), and other extracurricular activities.

That seemed like a lifetime ago.

A cat meowed loudly, startling her, and she jerked to a stop in the alley, peering around, suddenly feeling as if she wasn't as alone as she'd first thought. There was no one there but that didn't lessen the uneasy feeling.

Crossing her arms over her chest, she rubbed her upper arms, trying to chase away the sudden chill that came over her. It didn't help. As the hair on the back of her neck rose, she edged closer to one of the buildings, looking around for any signs of another person.

A black cat darted out from a pile of trash, making her jump in place and then burst into a fit of nervous giggles. She lowered her arms and stepped out and away from the building to continue in the direction of the bus stop.

Suddenly, pain exploded at the base of her skull. She knew she was falling but there was nothing she could do to stop it as darkness claimed her fully.

She wasn't sure how long she'd blacked out for. When she came to, her head felt as if she'd been hit with a bat. Morgan blinked and sat up slowly, disoriented and confused as to how she'd come to be on the ground.

"Hey there," said a familiar voice as a dark shadow appeared above her, making her breath catch. When the figure came into focus, she was totally and completely baffled as to why her godfather was there, bending over her.

"Luc?" she asked, thoroughly confused.

Why on earth was he outside of the concert venue at all, let alone at this time of night? And what had happened to her?

He forced a smile to his face. "Are you in any pain?"

"Pain? My head hurts. Why does my head…" Before she finished the sentence, she remembered running through the alleyway in hopes of making the last bus. Then the uneasy feeling coming over her a few seconds before pain exploded through the base of her head. "W-what happened? Why are you here? *How* are you here?"

With a sigh, he took hold of her elbow and helped her to her feet. He then positioned himself behind her and forced her to face forward. "We can discuss it all later. For now, we should go."

She had far too many questions to let the conversation end there. Morgan leaned and looked over her shoulder at what Luc was clearly trying to conceal.

As she saw what it was—or rather, who—her stomach knotted, and her brain reeled with denial at what she was seeing.

It couldn't be real.

Could it?

It was her body there on the cold, hard, unforgiving concrete.

Denial was the first thing to run through her mind, followed closely by panic. But before either had a chance to manifest externally, she found herself blurting out her first thought. "Dude, am I dead?"

Luc sighed and a tic started just under his right eye. He nodded and averted his gaze. "You are."

She couldn't seem to tear her gaze from the sight of her body on the ground. She looked peaceful, as if she were merely asleep, not standing outside of herself, looking down. "What happened?" she asked, her voice barely there.

"Something bad," returned Luc, trying to usher her down the alley away from her body.

"No," she said, sarcasm dripping from her voice. "You don't say."

He grunted. "Trust you to still be a handful even when newly departed."

Another thought hit her. "Hold the phone. I'm dead, right? So, I'm like a ghost?"

"Something like that, yes," supplied Luc, being as clear as mud.

She touched her temple to rub away the pending migraine. "Holy crap. Ghosts get headaches?"

Luc huffed. "Morgan, really. We need to go now. I'm breaking a lot of rules here with you. It's best we not linger."

"Breaking a lot of...hey, hold up, how are you seeing me? You can see and hear ghosts? Luc, have you been hiding a cool side all my life?"

His lips twitched. "I've hidden a few things from you, yes. Morgan, please. I need to get you clear of here before one of my siblings notices a reaper didn't come for your soul."

Her mind raced, and she latched on to his comment on siblings and souls. Her eyes widened more. "Holy crapola, are you like the Grim Reaper or something?"

Luc snorted. "Uh, no. I'm not a reaper."

"*A* reaper, as in there is *more* than one?" she questioned.

He groaned. "Most people would freak out but obey in a situation like this. Not ask a billion questions."

Morgan raised a brow. "I'm not like most girls."

"Don't I know it. Come on. We really need to go now. Michael will no doubt wonder why it is he can't sense me and come to investigate," said Luc, doing his best to get her down the alleyway.

Morgan pointed at her body as the reality of her situation set in. "I'm dead."

"Yes. We've already been over that," stated Luc.

She glanced around frantically.

"What are you doing now?" asked Luc.

"Looking for big creepy skeleton guys," she replied, before thinking they'd more than likely be in cloaks too.

Luc grunted. "They don't run around in robes. Well, not anymore. That's very old school."

She gasped. "You can read minds too?"

He took hold of her shoulder and all but pushed her down the alley. "No. Well, yes. But not yours. Some people are immune. You're one of them. I know you well enough to know where your head went when I said reaper."

"Blue Oyster Cult," she said quickly, nodding. "Right there and then straight for the cloaked figure."

He snorted.

Her gaze wandered back to her body— or at least to the spot her body *had* been. Her eyes widened. "Someone stole my body!"

Luc looked tired. "No. They didn't."

She pointed at the bare ground. "Yes they did!"

He took her by the elbow and hurried her down the alley more. He kept going with her before darting into a doorway of a side building as if he owned the place and went there often. It was pitch black inside. All of a sudden, there was an orange glow coming from Luc's hand. At first, she thought he had a flashlight with him—until she realized it was a ball of fire, and he was holding it.

Her eyes widened. "L-Luc?"

His shoulders slumped. "Morgan, I need you to stay calm when I tell you what I have to say."

"Highly unlikely, but carry on," she said, her mind feeling muddled as she was no doubt in shock.

"Here goes nothing," said Luc before facing her fully. "My full name is Lucifer."

Morgan lifted a brow as she stared at the ball of fire in his hand, putting together the name and the act. "Shut up! You're the devil? Like, *the devil?*"

He nodded and the flame vanished.

She grabbed him and turned him around.

He groaned. "I don't have a tail!"

"You so *do* read minds," she supplied.

He faced her and a soft light began to glow near them—this time it wasn't in his hand. She didn't need to be told that was his doing. "Morgan, there is a lot at work here that I don't want to get into with you right now. I need to get you somewhere no one can touch you or take your soul for now."

It all hit her hard. "W-what about me? Erm, my body? Someone body-jacked it. Is there some sort of bureau of the afterlife we can report a missing body to?"

He lifted a brow. "Your mind is a very strange place."

"Thanks. About the purgatory police," she stressed.

He sighed. "Your body wasn't stolen. *I* handled it."

She looked to the flame in his hand, and he instantly extinguished it somehow.

"I did not burn your body away. Stop looking at me like I did," he said.

"Mind reader," she chastised.

"You're rather exhausting to deal with," he said evenly with a slight smirk.

"Thanks."

Luc looked upward and sniffed the air. He growled slightly. "The Collective is sending more people here. They know by now the act is done, and they'll want your soul."

He turned his head and then led her back outside. He looked toward the end of the alley.

Morgan followed his gaze and gasped when she spotted the cowboy from the concert. She tensed. "Hot dude killed me?"

"What?" asked Luc quickly.

She stared at him while she pointed down at the end of the alley. "The cowboy. He's who killed me?"

Luc shook his head. "No."

She couldn't rip her gaze from the man at the end of the alley.

"You got her?" Cowboy asked.

"I do," returned Luc. "My word she'll be fine. That I'll personally watch over her until it's time."

"You better," warned the cowboy. "Is she there with you?"

Morgan was totally and completely lost. "Is who here? Did the Collectors kill someone else too?"

Luc snorted. "It's the Collective, not

collectors. And I'm sure they have, just no one other than you right here."

She touched her chest lightly. "Is he talking about me?"

"He is," said Luc.

Morgan thought harder on it. "Hold the phone. He, like, can't see me?"

Luc's mouth twitched. "No. He can't. Unless you want him to."

"How do I do that?" she asked.

"Just want it and it will happen," replied Luc.

Morgan took a deep breath and thought about the cowboy and how electrified she'd felt at the simple brush of his lips and about his words.

I love you.

They stuck in her head on a loop.

"Look at that, darlin'," he said from the end of the alley. "Here I've been upset you took so long to show yourself to me, and I'm pretty much the first person outside of Luc there to see you like this. Now, go with him. He'll keep you safe."

"W-who are you?" she asked.

Luc put up a hand. "No. She can't know

any more. Telling her more risks both of your futures."

"Lame, Luc. Lame," said Morgan, a nervous laugh escaping her.

Nodding, Luc took her arm. "We need to go now. I can't risk anything happening to your soul."

"But what about the cowboy?" asked Morgan, looking back to find the hunk was gone.

"Morgan, please," stressed Luc. "The Collective isn't something you want to go up against yet. You're not ready, and I'm only allowed to interfere so much. And I kind of already blew way past that limit, so let's go."

"Fine, but tell me who this Collective is."

He sighed. "A very bad group of people who make me look downright cuddly. It's enough to say your family has spent generations making pacts with them. It was time for a sacrifice to be made by your family. It was decided before you ever came to be that it would be you."

She thought of the contract she'd read that had required her parents have a child, and then kept referring to said child as a sacrifice. "W-what?"

He stilled. "Morgan, I'm sorry. Know that wasn't my doing. That I tried to steer them from the path of darkness."

She stared blankly at him. "But you said you're the devil."

"Yes," he replied. "Because I am."

"Then wouldn't you be trying to get more people on the evil train?" she asked.

He tipped his head. "It doesn't work that way. I oversee hell. That doesn't mean I'm evil."

"Doesn't mean you're not," she shot back quickly before thinking harder on it. She'd known him all her life. Nothing about him was evil or bad. "Sorry. That popped out."

"Don't apologize. I'm not a perfect person, Morgan. No one is. We all have shades of light and dark within us. Portions of good and evil. It's what we do with them that matters. I've known demons with hearts of gold and humans with hearts so dark, so twisted, that they'd be considered the monsters."

"Like my parents," she interjected.

He looked pained. "Yes and no. Muffy and Barton are products of their environments and their families. That being said, they had free will. They had the ability to change the agreement at any time by simply giving up their fortune."

Since she was dead and having an indepth conversation with the devil himself, Morgan didn't need it spelled out that her parents had decided against giving up their money to save her life. The proof was right before her eyes.

Her stomach sank. As much as she didn't want to believe what Luc was saying was true, it felt right.

"What about Booker and Spike? They need me," she said, her heart breaking for not only herself but her pets as well. Her bat and hedgehog needed tending.

Luc put a hand on her shoulder. "Morgan, they'll be fine. Millie will look after them. Not that they need her help."

She thought of Millie then. "I wish I could say goodbye to her."

"You'll see her again, one day," said Luc.

"In the meantime, she's where she needs to be. And I need to get you to where *you* need to be."

Gulping, she took a big breath. "I'm not going to cry right now. I'll do that later. For now, take me where it is you need to take me. And someday, you're going to explain who that hunk with the accent was."

Luc laughed. "As soon as I learn the details for myself. I think it's safe to say, time will tell."

Chapter Two

PRESENT DAY

New York (York) Peugeot fumbled with the volume of the sound system in his truck as he drove down a back road in his hometown of Hedgewitch Cove, Louisiana. He'd have taken a more direct route into the center of town if he wasn't having yet another rotten day with the vehicle. The biggest issue of the day was that the music it was currently blaring wasn't exactly anything he'd want anyone who knew him to hear.

The volume was currently set at a level that would let those in the neighboring state of Mississippi hear what he was playing, it was that loud. His hearing—that of a were-shark—was impressive to say the least. He certainly didn't need the volume jacked to eleven. It was set at two but that meant nothing. The truck's sound system had a mind of its own as of late, and currently it had decided to play music whether he wanted it on or not.

Late October meant the temperature was what some Yankees might term as tolerable, but York, who was a born and bred Southerner, thought it was a bit on the cool side. The humidity wasn't quite as thick as usual and that was a welcome relief, seeing as how the windows in his truck were stuck down. To make matters worse, the central air in his home was on the fritz as well. Didn't matter that the unit was only three years old.

Wouldn't be the first time in the last fifteen months that a piece of machinery, like a vehicle or home appliance, had basically gone nutty on him. Just the other day the blender had acted up. If it wasn't for the fast actions of Sigmund, his brother-in-law,

York would have two fewer fingers than he'd started with.

Typically, it was one of his boats breaking down. They'd done everything from stop running midtrip to begin to sink. The problem had been so bad that York had all but given up going out on a boat. It wasn't just that he loved being out on the open water; his family owned a large fishery, and York ran it.

Or at least, he *had* run it fully, until his grandmother had up and decided it was high time her grandchildren met their mates.

Her well-meaning gesture that had come in the form of a spell going awry had left each and every one of her grandchildren with a curse of chaos over their heads. Ever since, everything in York's life had been upside down.

His grandmother had meant well. And she'd certainly never expected to wrap the spell in a curse of chaos, but as luck would have it, she had. And chaos was precisely what York had endured since the spell—or curse, as he liked to refer to it—had taken place.

The only way to break the darned curse was to find their mates and actually claim them. Since claiming for a supernatural was far more than just getting married, that was saying something. There was no out when it came to claiming a mate.

No takebacks.

No do-overs.

And no such thing as divorce.

It was for keeps and forever.

He shuddered thinking about being tied down to just one woman for all eternity. What kind of man signed up for such a thing? There were so many beautiful women out there, just waiting to be romanced, who could settle on one?

He certainly couldn't.

Sure, he'd been going through something of a dry spell when it came to dating, but that was a direct result of the curse over his head. It was one thing to have his blender nearly bite his hand off but quite another to explain it away to a woman, or worse yet, have a piano fall on her head from being too close to him.

Already his identical twin, Louisiana (Louis), had narrowly escaped taking a piano to the head on three separate occasions. It was starting to become something of a running family joke. Though York suspected the joke would run out of funny real quick should it actually injure or kill Louis.

Sadly, it was just a matter of time before the spell went too far and cost someone their life. Everyone knew it, but no one was outright saying it.

Just this morning, York had gotten a call from Louis because something his brother deemed important had arrived at the antiques shop. Since Louis ran the shop for the family, and it was more than merely a place one stopped to buy antiques, people took note when anyone sounded the critical alarm. Especially when Louis said he'd taken whatever it was directly to the vault below the shop that contained magical artifacts entrusted to the care and oversight of the supernatural hunters. Since that was what York and his siblings were (something they got from their father's side of the family), it was their responsibility to keep a handle on things at the shop.

The music in the truck instantly cut out and York heard his cell phone ring. He pressed the button on his steering wheel that permitted the vehicle to connect with Bluetooth to his cell. "What's up?"

"What's up?" asked his father, his Cajun accent shining through. "That how your momma taught you to answer a phone?"

York chuckled. "I noticed you didn't mention how *you* taught me to answer one."

Walden Peugeot laughed loudly. "That's because I know darn well what you learned from me. Guess I should be happy you managed to be as civil as you were. Where you at?"

"About two miles out from Kelpie Lane," answered York. "Headed in to see Louis. He call you about the important thing-a-ma-jiggy?"

"He isn't excited about rare stamps again, is he?" asked Walden, a note of horror in his voice. Walden never really understood Louis to the extent he did York.

That was because York was cut from the same hellion cloth as his father. He'd deny as much, but it was the truth. York had heard more than one tale of his father's wild days before he'd met York's mother, Murielle Caillat, and settled down to have a family.

As York thought about the last time Louis had gotten worked up over stamps, he groaned. "I hope not. I didn't haul myself out of bed early to listen to him nerd out on me."

"Pull yourself out of bed early?" questioned Walden with a grunt. "It's nearly noon. Boy, tell me you didn't close the bar last night."

"All right. I didn't close the bar last night," said York.

His father let out an annoyed breath. "You lyin' to me, boy?"

"Nope. I was drinking on the pier with Blackbeard, Curt, Sigmund, and Leo." York waggled his brows for effect, despite the fact his father couldn't see him.

"I'm so proud," said his father snidely. "My son and sons-in-law were drunk as skunks in public."

"Could have been worse," reminded York as he continued to drive. "Could have been Momma, Mémé, and the rest of their social circle drinking on the docks. Remember when they did that last time? Mémé tried to stuff dollar bills in Blackbeard's jeans when he lifted her to carry her home."

Walden grunted. "Don't go reminding me about how all the women drool over that ghost."

"Daddy, ain't nothing ghost-like about Blackbeard. He's as present as you and me. And he's basically the Pied Piper of women. Trust me, I avoid heading out to places with chicks when I know he'll be there, because I know he'll get all the attention."

Walden said a few choice words on the matter before clearing his throat. "I called for a reason."

"I figured it wasn't to talk about Blackbeard's sex appeal."

"No," said Walden. "It wasn't. Luc reached out to me this morning asking if I'd seen the Box of Righted Wrongs."

York shook his head. "Who names these things?"

"No clue," said Walden. "All I do know is he's looking for it and sounded worked up."

"What's this Righted Wrongs thing do?" asked York, unsure he really wanted to know.

"From what I remember from my daddy when he mentioned it years ago, it has the power to open the door between the spirit realm and the human one."

"How do you mean?"

"I'm not exactly sure of the hows and whys myself. All I know is, the whispers about it say it ain't nothing good we'd want roaming about freely. In the wrong hands, a lot of damage could be done. Can you and Louis lend Luc a hand hunting for it? I'm gonna be tied up out here at Dead Man's Creek for hours yet."

"Can do," said York, a second before his father disconnected the call and the music began to blare once more from the sound system.

Hedgewitch Cove was certainly no stranger to the odd or to spirits. It had to be the most haunted town in America, if not the world. Most of its ghostly inhabitants were stuck within the confines of the town. Some couldn't even leave the property on which they'd died. Then there were others, a select few, who could come and go as they pleased. But outside the magical limits of the town, the ghosts weren't seen and heard with any kind of ease by humans.

He couldn't imagine what it would be like to go through life—or in their case, death—never being able to communicate with anyone. That had to be a lonely existence.

Instantly, he thought of Morgan, a spirit who lived at Hells Gate Inn. The place was owned and operated by Luc Dark. Luc's main job was a little bit bigger than just running an inn. He also happened to be the guy in charge of hell.

The devil himself.

Luc's place was full of the undead of all kinds, and just about every type of supernatural you could think of. York had once heard his mother refer to Luc's place as a halfway house for the wayward, and he had to admit that seemed to be the case.

Morgan had haunted (or whatever you wanted to call it) the inn since York was just a baby. He knew a little about her death. Mostly that it happened in the late '80s at a concert. But he didn't know the specifics, despite trying to pry the information from Morgan and Luc.

Both were tight-lipped on what had left her dead and inhabiting the inn. Unlike some of the spirits there, Morgan could move around town with ease. York had never asked if she could leave the town limits, but he got the sense she didn't want to go. That maybe Hedgewitch Cove felt safe to her.

All he *was* sure of was that the woman fascinated him. It actually bordered on obsession, and he knew as much.

He'd considered going out with a bunch of women to take his mind off Morgan, but he'd never actually gotten around to it.

As he tried to think about the last date he'd gone on, the stereo volume increased exponentially. He wasn't sure how the speakers weren't blown, or at the very least crackling. The music was painfully loud but crisp—and very, very '80s. If he was right, the song was by a band named Wham.

Regardless of who sang it, the song wasn't something York wanted pumping from his sound system as he drove through town with his windows stuck down.

But the curse had other ideas.

The music stopped suddenly.

"Interesting song choice," said a sultry female voice from next to him in the cab of the truck.

York jerked on the wheel and nearly went off into a ditch before he managed to right himself and the truck. He pulled off to the side of the road and put the car in park, his heart thundering.

"Where did you learn to drive?" asked the woman, who didn't show herself, but instead remained a disembodied voice to him. A voice he knew well.

Morgan.

She chuckled. "Didn't mean to scare you."

"What part of popping into my truck

out of thin air and talking to me without me knowing you're here wouldn't scare the living daylights out of me?" questioned York, pleased to have her near him, despite nearly wetting himself.

A half-drunk can of soda from the day prior rose by what looked like its own will. He knew better. Morgan was picking it up. "Eww. You drink this stuff? Gross. It's warm."

"It's from yesterday," he confessed.

The soda can floated in midair. "You really need to clean out your truck."

He'd have taken offense, but she was right. He did need to clean it. He kept a tidy house, even if it was decorated in what his sisters liked to refer to as the single man's furniture choices, but he wasn't so great about keeping his truck free of junk, namely, soda cans and food wrappers.

He looked over at the empty seat next to him, his mind filling in the void with a mental image he'd conjured of the woman. It was hot. Very hot. "Miss me?"

"Totally," she said with a soft laugh that made his entire body tighten. "Just checking in to see what trouble you're getting yourself into now. Wasn't expecting to find you jamming to Wham."

He smacked his lips together. "I'm a multifaceted man."

She laughed more. "*Sure* you are. Your grandmother's spell is controlling your music choices again, isn't it?"

He offered a bad-boy grin. "Yep. Did the sound of '80s music draw you to me? If so, I'm going to play it all the time."

She set the soda can down in the drink holder once more. "It's like a dog whistle to me."

"Really?" he asked, making a mental note to buy every song from the decade and blare it every chance he got.

She snorted. "No. It doesn't work that way."

He cut the engine and continued to look in the direction he sensed her in. "How does it work? Were you really just wanting to check in to see if I was up to no good?"

"Hon, I assume you're always up to no good," she said.

Hon.

He liked hearing her refer to him in such a manner.

"Admit it, you just came to see me because you missed me. I've grown on you," he said, hoping his words were true.

She nudged him lightly. "Kind of like a rash."

"Hey, I'll take it," he returned, reaching out as if to caress her. The only problem was, he didn't know exactly where she was or what he might touch on her.

For a split second it felt as if her finger grazed his, but that couldn't be. It would have meant she wanted to hold his hand. That couldn't be right. Could it?

She growled lightly and the sound was nothing short of adorable. "I have to go. Betty and Bob are stirring up some trouble. I promised to keep an eye on them for Luc."

"Stay," he said fast before trying to play it ultra-cool. Somehow, he was reasonably sure he failed. "Um, I mean, I'm sure they're fine. How much trouble can one demon and one ornery spirit get into?"

As he asked the question, he realized the answer and sighed. "You should go. Now."

She laughed, and the sound was much closer than he expected. The next thing he knew, the smallest of chaste kisses was placed upon his cheek, and he stiffened, afraid to move for fear he'd scare her away from ever doing such a thing again.

When, in reality, he wanted her to do that and much, much more.

"Morgan?" he asked with a gasp, only to find he was once again alone in the cab of the truck.

York's hand went to his cheek, to the spot where she'd kissed him. That wasn't something she'd ever done before. Sure, it was chaste, but it was still a kiss.

He was about to dwell on it more when his truck and the music kicked back on, this time louder than ever.

With a groan, he put it into gear and drove out onto the road once more. His thoughts were still on Morgan as he neared the more populated area of town.

A quick glance over at a huge white antebellum home showed him that he'd not gone unnoticed. Three of the women from his momma's bridge group were there, each sitting in a white rocking chair, each fanning themselves with small paper fans in one hand while holding what he could only guess was sweet tea in the other.

From the disapproving look on Mrs. Schulyer's face, York's mother would be getting an earful sooner rather than later.

He offered a curt wave and went faster than he should have, his sights set on the upcoming turnoff for Kelpie Lane. The street ran past his sister's magic shop and fed into the main artery of downtown Hedge-witch Cove.

Just when he thought it couldn't possibly get worse, he turned onto Kelpie Lane as a man in a dark rain slicker with a matching surrey hat walked right out in front of him (nowhere near the crosswalk).

The music in the truck cut off instanta-neously.

Tires squealed as York slammed on the brakes, gripping the wheel to the point he nearly ripped it from the dash. The vehicle came to a stop just shy of striking the male.

The man still fell over, vanishing from York's view.

York fumbled with his seat belt to get it off and hurried from the truck, leaving the driver-side door standing wide open.

"Good Lawd!" exclaimed a Cajun-tinged voice from the back of one of the houses on the street. "York done went and killed Arnie."

There, lying on the street in front of the truck, was a man clad head to toe in dark colors. He had on his ever-present rain slicker and the board sign that he wore around his neck. It usually covered the man's front and back with sayings that all revolved around the end of days. It was how he'd gotten the nickname of Apocalypse Arnold. Right now, the front of the sign was popped up, covering Arnold's face and head.

York held his breath as he bent quickly to check on Arnold. He'd thought he hadn't hit the man, but now he wasn't so sure.

"Is he dead?" asked Barnebas Cybulski, his mailbag cast aside near the edge of the road as he rushed over to assist. Since Barnebas was also a volunteer firefighter in addition to being the town's mail carrier, his help was more than welcome.

York's hand made contact with the wood sign just as Arnold moaned.

"Am I dead?" questioned Arnold from under the sign.

Barnebas rolled his eyes. "I already asked that question, Arnie."

York lifted the sign and made an attempt to ease the strap over Arnold's head. He wanted to check the man over to be sure he was indeed as fine as he sounded. That earned him a swat to the arm from Arnold before the man grabbed hold of the sign for dear life, his eyes wide.

"Don't go taking it from me. I'll be naked," said Arnold.

"Naked? You're fully dressed and in a rain slicker," corrected York. "We haven't seen a drop of rain in weeks and the weatherman ain't calling for any. I think you can probably take the sign off for a spell, and maybe the rain slicker too."

Barnebas muscled York out of the way, which was saying something, since the mailman was hardly someone anyone would put money on winning a fight. He took hold of Arnold and pulled him upright, helping to fix his surrey hat, which was cockeyed.

Reaching down, Arnold lovingly caressed his sign, assuring it was well. He let out a long, slow breath, his eyes sad. "I thought it was the end. I saw the sign."

Barnebas scratched the back of his head. "Like the big white light? Like your maker?"

Arnold appeared puzzled. "No," he said, tapping the sign. "I literally saw the sign. This one here. Figured I was a goner."

"Sorry to disappoint, but you're still among the living," said Barnebas, pulling York's full attention to him. It was then York realized the mail carrier was wearing a pair of boxer shorts with a postage stamp pattern and a T-shirt with an eagle on it. The flip-flops he'd paired with them really drove home just how odd the man was.

"Didn't the town council ban you from wearing your skivvies to deliver the post?" asked York, distinctly recalling a town meeting devoted entirely to the subject of Barnebas and his attempts to wear his underwear to work.

Barnebas grinned. "Got these as a

birthday present from the district supervisor. So, they're government issued. Loophole."

"I really need to consider moving somewhere sane," said York, partially under his breath. He didn't mean it. Doing so would mean he'd be away from his family and Morgan.

Barnebas grinned. "You wouldn't get far. You're not like your siblings, Arizona or Georgia. Hedgewitch Cove suits you perfect. I can't picture you somewhere fancy, like say, New York City. You'd never make it out there among the humans."

At the mention of humans, Arnold shivered and clutched his bell and sign tighter. "They're scary."

Barnebas nodded. "They sure are. Did you hear another one managed to get through the town wards?"

A spell had been cast over the town at its inception to help keep humans from wandering in and invading the haven for supernaturals. Every once in a while, a human made it past the wards that normally compelled them to keep on driving, to not notice the town at all, and to never put it on a map. As of late, more and more humans were eking through. It was certainly cause for concern.

After all, supernaturals weren't known to humans.

Arnold looked upward. "Humans are invading. The end really is near."

"Well, now, I don't know that I'd go to that extreme, but something is amok," stated Barnebas.

York stood and rotated his neck and stretched his shoulders some. He towered over the other two males. Not really a surprise, since his father was just shy of seven feet tall. "You okay, Arnold?"

"No. Humans are coming for us all," said the man before he began to ring his bell, going on and on about the end being near.

Barnebas snorted. "He's fine. You scared him. That's all. I'll keep an eye on him and lift his spirits some by reminding him we've got jazz band practice this week for the upcoming Dead Rising Day parade. You excited? It'll be my first one. You?"

The question would have been peculiar,

seeing as how the day came about once every one hundred years, but many residents in the town had seen way more years than just a hundred. Immortality was fairly common around these parts.

"Yep, I'll be there. But I'm not sure what all the fuss is about," he said, secretly looking forward to the day. It was a time when spirits could walk the Earth in human form for twenty-four hours. And he had one spirit in mind that he'd been waiting all his life to meet face-to-face.

Barnebas eyed him closely. "Hmm, so there isn't a sassy young lady who just happens to live over at Hells Gate Inn whom you'd like to spend some quality time with that day?"

"Nope," answered York, as his deep voice cracked slightly. It took all he had not to reach up and touch the spot Morgan had kissed. "Just another day to me. Not sure why we've had to have a month-long cele-bration in anticipation of it."

"Uh-huh," murmured Barnebas. "Keep telling yourself that. Maybe you'll even believe it soon enough."

York pretended not to notice the comment.

Barnebas motioned to York's truck. "Didn't realize you liked George Michael so much."

"Like George who…?" York thought about the music that had been blaring from his truck. He groaned. "Love him. Can't get enough."

"So I heard." Barnebas went for his discarded mailbag. "I need to get back to work. You take care now not to run over anyone else."

York went back to his open truck door and climbed in. The moment his backside touched the seat, the music began to play loudly once more.

Barnebas shook his head.

York did his best to appear fine with the music selection. He even attempted to tap along to the beat. He had nearly no rhythm. The song started once more and began to skip, repeating something about doing the jitterbug over and over again.

York grunted and kept driving. If he didn't get to the antiques shop that his brother ran for the family, Louis would send out the troops and have a major-sized melt-down. That was just Louis's way.

Explaining to Louis that the morning had been one calamity after another would get York nowhere.

He tuned out the blaring music as he drove, continuing to think about Morgan. The woman had been showing up at random much more frequently as of late, and while he had to admit he was thrilled by the fact, it also confused him. Much like the kiss had. Most of the time, she razzed him, and he did the same to her, as if they were best friends who enjoyed getting the better of one another. But there was something more there, on his side at least. Something he couldn't put his finger on, and before the chaste kiss, he'd have bet money on the fact it was one-sided.

Now he wasn't so sure.

Then again, it wasn't as if she'd ever even shown herself to him.

No.

She reserved that for a select few chosen

ones, and York apparently wasn't on that elite list.

It was hard not to take offense since she'd shown herself to pretty much everyone he knew.

He had a mental image of her, brought about from what others said she looked like. He wasn't sure how close or how far he was from what she actually looked like, and he didn't care. He liked being near her, even if he couldn't see her. She got his sense of humor and had a dry wit about her that he enjoyed and looked forward to. Of course, on most days he assumed he just annoyed her. Then again, she'd kissed his cheek today.

That was something.

Part of him had to admit that he went out of his way to get under her skin because he enjoyed her reactions and simply having a reason to talk to her. The sound of her voice had always been soothing to him and his inner beast. The shark side of him was often restless, wanting to be out in the ocean, not stuck on dry land.

Morgan's voice had a way of staving off

issues with his shark, calming it nearly instantly when she spoke—even if she was yelling at him.

Absently, his hand found his cheek once more, easing over the spot she'd kissed on his scruffy jawline.

Damn if the woman didn't have a way of twisting him all up inside.

Chapter Three

MORGAN STOOD with her arms folded under her chest, shaking her head slightly as Bob, an Earthbound spirit who resided at Hells Gate Inn, hovered near the desk in Luc's study, encouraging the elderly woman sitting there to go ahead with her newest online purchase. It all seemed harmless enough, until one took into consideration the sweet older woman he was helping was really a demon, and the purchase they were trying to make was zombie body parts—in bulk.

She wasn't exactly thrilled to have to return to the inn to keep a handle on Betty and Bob, especially since she'd been spending a little time with York. The strangest urge to go to him had come over her out of the blue, and she'd listened to it, popping into his truck. Seeing him was always something of a highlight of her day, but she didn't dare admit that out loud to anyone.

Her fingers went to her lips as she thought about the kiss she'd given him quickly before returning to the inn. It had been impulsive to a point because whenever she was close to him, she struggled with the urge to make contact with him in some manner. Finally, she'd given in and done just that.

"That button there," said Bob to Betty, yanking Morgan from her thoughts on York.

They'd been down the road of Bob assisting Betty with internet purchases more than once in recent years, and each time Luc had been less than pleased with the results. They'd only just gone through all the were-wolf toes Betty had ordered with Bob's help. They'd been used by her in countless family recipes (that only she and her sisters ate) and as dog treats for the hellhound that also resided on the premises.

Three of Betty's five sisters had arrived in town for an impromptu family reunion some eight months prior and had yet to leave. They'd oddly fit right in to Hedge-witch Cove. They weren't full-time residents of Hells Gate, like Betty was, but they weren't totally unsupervised either, thanks to Luc's insistence that they stay at the retire-ment center near the edge of town.

Thunderbird Estates had areas for those who needed round-the-clock care or just some supervision, and a large section for those who didn't require much in the way of health needs. Since the sisters were as old as time but healthy, they technically could be in the retirement section, not the assisted-living quarters. But they weren't exactly saints, so that hadn't worked out as planned.

Especially since Luc had forgotten to forbid them from eating staff members.

So, after a rather unfortunate incident that resulted in the need for the center to hire two new male nurses, several more groundskeepers, and a new cook, they now knew the rules.

Morgan found them amusing and popped in to visit them often. Even though they were demons, they were a functional family in comparison to hers, which was saying something.

Upon her death, and after learning that her parents had been heavily involved in what sounded more and more like a cult to her every day, Morgan had refrained from asking Luc for additional details on them. She didn't want to hear about how they'd selected money and power over their only child. Hearing it once was more than enough to last her for all eternity. And while she could come and go as she pleased, unlike many of the spirits in town, the burning need to go home—back to New York City— had never come over her.

While she'd grown up loving the city and everything about it, the taint of dying there was something she carried with her to this very day. Then there was the fact the town she now called home had grown on her tremendously. This was a good place. A safe place, even with most of the Sisters Six (what Betty and her sisters had been nick-named by Luc). And here was where her godfather called home for the most part. He liked to say it was one of many homes he owned, and it was, but it was the place he laid his hat on most occasions.

Morgan, Luc, and the rest of the people who lived at the inn were something of a family. Hells Gate Inn inhabitants ranged from the living-challenged to the devil himself. At first, it had been mind-blowing to Morgan when Luc had brought her there directly after her death. Not only had she needed to come to terms with being deceased and learning supernaturals were a real thing, but she'd also needed to learn to adjust to life in a small Southern town. Hedgewitch Cove was about as different from New York City as one could get, yet she'd fallen for its quirky charm and its residents.

Even Bob, who was always up to no good.

If it wasn't for the fact Bob was basically levitating behind Betty, no one would have known the man was a spirit. From his balding head with white hair around the sides and back—that matched the white hairs that sprouted forth from his ears, as well as his bushy eyebrows—to his rosy, rounded cheeks, he looked alive. He'd died in his late sixties, and from what Morgan had been able to gather, had been something of a mischief-maker in life as in death.

The man liked to reminisce about better days when things were more straightforward, and when he'd have been allowed to smoke anywhere he wanted. Since he'd died during the 1950s, that made sense. He'd died of lung cancer, which also made sense. Didn't stop him from taking every opportunity he could to plant himself in the path of anyone who happened to be smoking.

Since the act wasn't permitted within the inn, Bob spent a lot of time outside whenever a guest who was a smoker stayed. He was bound to the inn, meaning he couldn't actually leave the grounds. For the best, since he would have wreaked havoc all over town.

Betty, who was a few inches shy of five feet, making her very tiny indeed, was sitting in Luc's executive office chair, on a throw pillow to boost her up. She had on a pale lavender pantsuit with matching slip-on flats. Her short hair was curled the same as it always was. She had on a gold brooch that looked like a flower until one examined it closer and realized it was a demon with its mouth open wide, showing rows upon rows of jagged teeth.

It was one of many from her collection of bizarre and dark jewelry. It had been a gift from Luc, and she cherished it, never letting it out of her sight for too long. For as disturbing as most would find the item, Morgan had to admit she liked it. Then again, she'd always been attracted to darker items.

When she'd passed, she'd been considered punk or even goth, depending on who you asked, but going off today's standards and labels, she'd have been called emo more than likely. Yes, her tastes had evolved somewhat over the years, but she still liked and gravitated toward the macabre. Thankfully, unlike some spirits, she wasn't stuck wearing the same thing she'd passed in. She had the ability to change what she appeared in, but not with the same ease that Bob did. Bob simply thought it and it was.

Not Morgan.

She had to get dressed, but she could at least make the clothing vanish with her whenever she didn't want to be seen. She had a room at the inn and it was furnished just as if she were alive. The closet had articles of clothing and various shoes for her to select from, and she had to physically change into them, rather than simply wishing it so. It was wrong to be jealous of dead people, but even she had to admit the ability to think it and make it a reality was pretty neat.

Today she'd gone with a pair of dark skinny jeans, black soft-leather knee-high boots, a long-sleeved black and white checked, button-up shirt, and a gray cardigan sweater over it. The shirt and the sweater hung to her mid-thigh, looking a lot like a dress. She had on full makeup, something else she had to do by hand each day, and her shoulder-length hair was down, its trademark red streak in the front.

That was something that didn't change.

The red streak.

She used to have to dye it when she was alive, to give contrast to her otherwise ink-black hair, but that had changed in death. Her hair grew, just as it would if she were alive, forcing her to get haircuts, but the red streak was now permanent. At least that was what Medusa, the woman who owned and operated the beauty salon in town, had told her. Medusa had also mumbled something about Morgan being different than most of the dead but hadn't elaborated further.

"Buy it, Betty," encouraged Bob, sounding gleeful. He knew he was up to no good.

Betty lifted her small hand and put it on the mouse for the computer. "I hit this then?"

"Click," corrected Morgan from the background. "It's called clicking."

She nodded and kept her gaze locked on the screen. "I do so love to hit things."

And she did.

While she may have appeared to be mild-mannered and meek even, she could more than hold her own. In fact, she was downright deadly when the need called for it. Sometimes even when it didn't.

Morgan strongly suspected that was part of the reason Luc had her living at the inn rather than roaming free in hell like the rest of her family and friends. She was something of a liability and could quickly get herself into a pickle that would leave her being targeted by demon hunters.

While the woman did, at times, get herself into some precarious positions, Morgan didn't want her harmed. It was why she helped to keep an eye on her for Luc. And what Betty was doing now would surely get Luc's dander up.

With a sigh, Morgan eased forward slightly. "Betty, I don't think you need to order zombie parts. You know Jasmine offered to bring you some from New Orleans when she gets back from her trip there. Not to mention, Luc isn't going to be happy."

New Orleans was just a hop, skip, and a jump from Hedgewitch Cove, which made sense, since it had such a sizeable supernatural community itself. It was one of the most haunted cities in the world. Hedgewitch

Cove was right up there with it. Case in point, Morgan, Bob, and the countless other spirits who called it home.

"Oh, that Jasmine is such a dear, real shame she's been spending so much time with that hunter boy," said Betty in a soft voice. "You know his people hunted my people, and his kin, way back when, they killed some of my family."

The hunter boy at the center of the conversation was none other than Leopold "Leo" Gibbons. He'd come to town with Curt Warrick and Petey Williams a while back and had yet to leave. Currently, Leo had been assisting Louis with running the antiques shop next to Hells Gate while the owner dealt with a rather nasty but well-meaning curse.

Betty's feet, which did not touch the floor due to her small stature and Luc's large chair, swung as if she were a small giddy child. In many ways, she was.

"Always thinking of me, that Jasmine," said Betty as she glanced up briefly from the computer screen. "You know, just the other day she promised to bake cookies with me. I just love to bake. These zombie parts would be here just in time for the celebration. My sisters and I could make so many wonderfully delicious goodies to share with the town."

"Betty," said Morgan, "Jasmine won't let you put anything out of the ordinary into the cookies. And what celebration?"

"Out of the ordinary?" questioned Betty, her voice raising slightly. "I'll have you know I've been making cookies with zombie parts for centuries. To me, any other way is out of the ordinary. You young folks just haven't developed a taste for the finer things. You should try Leva-Joyce's scones made with zombie-parts flour. It's gluten-free."

Morgan hoped she never did get a taste for zombie parts or werewolf toes. And there was no way she would ever eat anything Betty's sisters made either. They were too much like her.

She was very pleased she didn't need to eat or drink at all. Especially not with as much as Betty had been trying to sneak in extra ingredients as of late. Though Morgan did have to admit she missed the ability to taste food and enjoy it. Too many days she'd spent catching the scent of the sweets from the bakery just down the street. Her mouth practically watered for them, but she'd learned long ago there was very little point to bothering. She could no longer taste them, which took from the enjoyment of the act. Plus, she didn't actually get hungry, and eating to just eat was pointless.

Bob glanced at Morgan and grinned mischievously. "Don't listen to her, Betty. You can never have too many zombie parts."

Nodding, Betty clicked a button on the screen that allowed her to instantly purchase what she wanted. "Oh, I agree. Good to stock up on them. You never know when there will be a shortage. You know, during the depression, they were much harder to come by. For a while there, they were rationed just like ghoul bits were. And during prohibition, it was so very hard to come by quarts of good blood. The vampires and the demons would stage the best sit-ins. Those were the days."

Morgan rubbed her temple, the pair of

them making her tired. "Luc won't be happy about this."

Bob waggled his bushy brows. "I know."

"You know you should not encourage her," she warned Bob.

Betty waved a hand dismissively. "Luc will be just fine. Besides, he has more pressing matters to deal with. Such as Dead Rising Day, and then there is that whole thing involving you, dear."

Morgan stiffened. "What thing involving me?"

Bob cleared his throat, his loafer-covered feet touching the floor. "*Nothing*. You know how she is. She forgets and gets things confused. Happens when you're as old as time." His attention shifted rather awkwardly back to Betty. "How old are you again, Betty?"

"Hmm, how old is the Earth?" she returned.

"Old," offered Bob.

Betty nodded. "It is. I still remember when Belial and I were an item. Warriors made my three hearts beat so fast."

Three hearts?

That was news to Morgan.

Tipping her head, Betty looked far off in thought. "My sister Mildred tried to steal Belial from me. We were always competing back then to see who could impale the most or make our torture victims scream the loudest. You know, the fun stuff. Any-who, she knew I was sweet on Belial. All the girls were. I mean, he was one of the first demons to get his name out there. But I digress. About Mildred. I fixed her a good one. I set her up on a blind date with an archangel."

"I'd love to meet Mildred at some point," said Morgan.

Betty eyed her. "Who said you haven't already met her?"

Bob was right. Betty did tend to get easily confused and easily mixed up.

Morgan glanced at the huge, ornate grandfather clock that was done in black with ravens carved into the wood. "Betty, you should rest. You were up before the sun again."

"Sweet dear, I was created before there was light. Makes sense I'd wake before it." Betty turned in the office chair and Bob assisted her with getting down. She took the throw pillow from the seat of the chair and walked it slowly over to the deep red Victorian sofa that sat against the far wall. She carefully returned the pillow to what had been its original position and then faced Morgan. "Yes, dear, it's hard to sleep at my age, but then again, I still manage to sleep more than you. But that will change soon enough."

Morgan didn't bother to question the statement because she knew Betty wasn't altogether home upstairs any longer.

Bob took her arm gently. "Um, Betty, Morgan is right. Let's get you up to your room for a nice nap."

With that, the two of them headed from the room just as Luc was entering. His gaze went to his laptop, which was open and on, still showing the shopping site Betty and Bob had been on. He sighed. "What did they do now?"

Morgan grinned. "Zombie parts. Don't worry, I made a point of saying you'd be unhappy."

"Bet that only encouraged Bob more,"

he said, as the edges of his mouth drew upward.

"It did," added Morgan. "You know him well."

Luc went to his computer and closed the lid. "I do. And I know he's excited about his first Dead Rising Day. I'm almost afraid to know what trouble he'll manage to get into while in human form for an entire day."

"Should be just enough time for him to burn Hedgewitch Cove to the ground accidentally, or on purpose," said Morgan, only partially joking. "On a good note, Howie is in hell visiting his mother again, so the dynamic duo will not be together for the event. How is his mother doing?"

Howie, a demon who just happened to be Morgan's best friend, and who was scared of anything happy, had been making frequent trips to hell to see his mother. She was getting older (as in, born-at-the-dawn-of-time kind of old) and was in poor health. Since his mother was like he was when it came to happy things, the fact she was nearing the end of her days somehow made Howie's entire family want to throw a party—his mother included. They were a strange lot for sure, but they cared about one another so that was all that mattered.

"She's feeling much better," said Luc. "Which means they're all now miserable and worried."

Morgan couldn't help but laugh. Being afraid of happy things was so bizarre, yet she'd gotten used to that and so many other things since her death.

Luc went to the far bookcase and began moving items around, obviously searching for something. "You haven't happened to have seen a small wooden box with two crescent moons, three stars, and a pentagram burned on the top, have you?"

Morgan thought on it. "No, but you have a lot of things with moons and pentagrams on them."

With a grin that the ladies no doubt found irresistible, he chuckled. "Sort of my thing. Doodled it once on heaven's version of a dinner napkin and it kind of stuck."

She aided in the search of his office for a box fitting the description. "Please tell me this isn't one of those end-of-the-world boxes. I hate it when you lose those."

He lifted a brow smugly. "I'll have you know I've only lost three of those in my lifetime. And then there was the one I left in a safe place only to have Pandora open it. Not my fault."

"Uh-huh, sure. Bet all the demonic world leaders say that," teased Morgan as they continued to look for the box. "So what does this one do?"

He tensed. "Nothing."

She stared at him. "That was almost believable. You know, you're rumored to be a great liar. It's like whoever wrote the stuff about you in the bible never even met you. Had they, they would have realized you're kind of the worst liar ever."

"Am not," argued Luc, sounding like a child. "My brother Gabriel is. I'm a close second though."

Laughing, she continued the search, vanishing quickly as she went to the closet and searched it before reappearing in the study. "It's not in there."

"Attic?" he asked.

She popped to the attic in the blink of an eye and searched with a speed only a spirit could before appearing in front of Luc once more. "Nope. Is there a spider in my hair? I'm sure I went through at least six cobwebs."

"No. There is no spider in your hair," he said, reaching out quickly and plucking one off her shoulder.

"Jerk."

"Most fear me," he said with a snort.

"Most don't have you as a godfather," she supplied, earning her another laugh from him. "When was the last time you saw the box?"

He rubbed his chin. "Nineteen eighty-nine."

The year stuck out to her for more than one reason. Namely, it was the year she'd died. "And it's suddenly imperative you have the box now?"

"It is."

"What does it do?" she questioned once more.

He licked his lower lip and then sighed. "It has the power to bring the dead to life."

She touched the bridge of her nose. "And this is something you left lying around for any old person to happen upon? Luc, what if Bob found it? Or worse yet, one of the spirits who haunt the Dead Forest? You want one of them roaming around alive again?"

She shuddered at the thought.

It took her a moment to realize Luc was staring at her oddly.

"Is there another spider on me?" she asked, before turning in several fast circles, working herself up to a scream.

He caught her shoulders, stopping her. "Morgan, there are no more spiders on you."

"Then why were you looking at me like that?"

"Because you haven't once hinted at wanting to use the box for yourself," he confessed.

She thought harder on it. "Why would I?"

"You don't miss being alive?" he asked, sadness touching his voice. "You were supposed to live a very long, very full life. What your parents did cut that short."

She tensed and waved a hand in the air dismissively. "I don't want to talk about it."

"You never want to discuss it." Luc stepped back from her. "It's okay to get upset and to be mad at what they did to you."

"Would that fix anything?" she asked, already knowing the answer. "I'd end up one of those bitter spirits in the forest. The ones that can't be trusted. I don't want that."

He sighed. "Morgan, Dead Rising Day is coming."

She lowered her gaze. "I know I'm not exactly like the rest of the spirits in town. I'm guessing that means it won't work the same for me as it does them."

"No," he confirmed. "It won't work the same."

A pang of sorrow came over her and she quickly tried to push it deep down, into the compartment where she kept her feelings locked away. "I understand. It will be nice for Bob and the others, having a day to be alive. I can pop around town to be sure they aren't getting into too much trouble for you, if you want."

Luc swallowed hard. "Can you do me a favor and pop over to the antiques shop? If memory serves, I think I might have entrusted one of the Peugeots with the box decades ago. I bet it's on a shelf down in the artifact area."

It took her a second to respond, as she fought the urge to give in to her emotions. "Yes. Of course. I'll be right back."

With that, she popped away from the inn and directly into the antiques shop.

Chapter Four

YORK PULLED his truck into an open space in front of the antiques shop and put it in park. As he did, the volume level of the music coming from his speakers managed to somehow get louder.

Cherry Corduas stepped out of the bookstore that was next to the shop and looked up at him, raising a brow as she did. The woman—who looked to be middle-aged, but who York suspected was older than that—shook her head as she mouthed something in his direction.

He shut off the truck, but the radio kept going.

Cherry waved a hand and just like that,

the music cut off. Her magic drifted over the air, making the gifts York had inherited from his mother's side respond in kind. His magic flared slightly but since it wasn't his main gift, he held his breath, hoping nothing disastrous occurred.

Thankfully, it didn't.

Blissful silence was all that remained.

York got out of his truck and made it to the sidewalk as Cherry continued to mouth something in his direction. He wondered if she'd taken to miming what she was trying to tell him. Why on earth didn't she just say it? Why mouth it?

It hit him then that the music had been so loud, he couldn't hear her speaking.

He motioned to his ears and shook his head.

She smiled and then waved her hand again. Her power trickled over him, helping him hear once more.

A natural-born witch, Cherry held a lot of power. Her family line had been some-what questionable in its usage of said power, but Cherry was working hard to change that image and show the town there was good in the Corduas line after all.

York was too young to have been around when the Corduas line was at its worst, but to hear his grandmother tell the tale, the family had been into some dark stuff. Looking at Cherry, who was currently wearing a neon-pink dress that hung nearly to the ground and had small blue flamingos on it, it was hard to picture her or her kin being anything close to evil.

She turned her head slightly, and her upswept hair showed off beach ball dangling earrings. Upon closer inspection, he realized the words "beach party" were printed on them in a small font. They matched her colorful glasses frames, which were very cat-eyed in their shape. Basically, the woman was about as eccentric as they came. Yet she fit right in with many of the inhabitants of Hedgewitch Cove.

And nothing about her screamed darkness and evil. If anything, she came off as carefree and happy in her dress and manner. That didn't change the way many in the town looked at her through a tainted lens.

She was still held accountable in many of
their eyes for the sins of her forefathers. It
was a shame some were so set in their ways
that they couldn't see how ignorant they
were being in judging her and her sisters so
harshly. From what York had been told,
Cherry hadn't been part of all the wrong-
doing her family had done. Neither had her
sisters, Lemon and Peach.

But they bore the name Corduas and
had their ancestors' magic running through
their veins. And for some, that was more
than enough to judge them guilty.

"That better, sugar?" she asked, her
drawl as Southern as they came.

York didn't have much room to talk
when it came to accents. He knew his was
thicker than most but not as thick as some in
town. He blamed his father for some of the
thicker parts. Walden Peugeot was Cajun
through and through.

Their mother liked to say, you can take
your daddy from the swamp, but you'll never
take the swamp from your daddy. That had
been true in more ways than one, seeing as
how Walden was also a were-gator.

York nodded his thanks to Cherry. "Thank you. Not sure what you did but you're tops on my list of people today, Miss Cherry."

She pursed her lips a tad. "Am I to assume you did not try to run over Arnie on the way into town?"

York groaned. There was nothing quite like the rumor mill of a tiny town. By the time dinner rolled around, the word on the street would be that Arnold was dead and gone, or worse.

"I didn't even bump him," returned York. "I did scare him."

Ms. Cherry looked to be fighting a grin. "Bet he was disappointed you didn't do him in. You know how much he's looking forward to the end."

"Well, he did get to see the sign," said York with a snort.

One of her over-plucked eyebrows darted upright in a questioning manner. "Do I want to know?"

"Nope. Probably not," said York. "I better get in there and see what Louis wanted me to stop by the shop for. You know how he gets when I take too long to do anything."

"Oh magic above, that boy is coiled tighter than a lawn mower's startin' string. Not nearly as bad as Virginia though," said Ms. Cherry with a slight whistle. "I really hope the twins are easier going like their father. I'm not sure the town can take another Type A personality. It's so…Northern."

It was said as the insult she meant it to be.

York couldn't help but chuckle at the mention of his sister, who was expecting twin boys any day now. "With me as an uncle, I'm sure everything will be fine. I get to spoil 'em real good, and then run away to leave my sister to handle the aftermath. Perfect. Just like I do with Missi's little one."

Ms. Cherry lowered her glasses slightly and peered down the end of her nose at him. "Joke will be on you when it's you havin' little ones before you know it."

He threw up his fingers, making the sign of a cross in an attempt to ward off her curse.

She laughed long and hard before heading down the street in the direction of the flower shop. "Gonna happen soon, *New York*. Real soon."

He paled, instantly feeling sweaty. "How soon we talking here? How many years?"

"Years?" she echoed with a broader grin as she glanced back at him. "Sweetie, we're talking months before your little ones start arrivin'."

He felt faint. "Months before I have little ones? But I haven't even met my mate."

She winked. "Who's to say you haven't already met them in some form or another? You've really got to learn to see with more than your eyes."

With that, she walked away, leaving him standing there, feeling as if he might very well pass out.

Chapter Five

"BROTHER?" York hurried down the stairs that led to the basement of the antiques shop and stopped just outside the closed, solid metal door. The door was ornate with all of its exposed cogwheels, and shades of golds and browns. While it looked to be a nod to steampunk, in reality it far predated the craze. It had been created by hunters and bespelled to help protect the contents within the vault. The vault was massive and defied logical, as did just about everything else about the enormous basement.

Walden had sat the boys down when they were younger and explained both the basement and their expected duties as born hunters in detail. Problem was, Louis had been the only one paying attention. York had been fixated on Morgan, who had been hovering near them a lot at the time, seeing as how the Collective had made an attempt on one of York's sisters not long prior.

Morgan had volunteered to keep an extra eye on York and his siblings until the proper spells could be put in place. While she'd not shown herself to York, he'd still been totally swept up with the idea of her. Though with age came different feelings. Ones he didn't exactly like to dwell upon.

What kind of man had the hots for a ghost?

A woman he'd never even seen?

York put his hand to a flat spot on the door and it began to glow with a faint yellow light. The cogwheels turned and the bolts holding the door in place disengaged. The door popped open, and he stepped through to find his twin standing before a large grouping of boxes, all of which were open.

Next to Louis was Petey Williams. While the older man was technically a town founder, he wasn't from the area. He was a

Yankee but an honorary local all the same. He was in his standard fishing waders with dark jeans beneath, and a flannel shirt. Didn't matter how hot out it was. He also had on a knit cap that barely contained his unruly gray hair.

"Petey? Louis?" asked York. "What's with all the boxes?"

It all looked like items that belonged in a vintage clothing shop, not the antiques store. In fact, most of it reminded him of the '80s.

Louis, who was in a pullover shirt with a collar and a pair of dress slacks (clothing York wouldn't be caught dead in), bent before another of the boxes and stared up at York, his dark eyes wide. "Look."

Petey put his thumbs through the suspenders of his waders and rocked on the balls of his feet as York walked around the boxes to stand near his brother.

"Can't you just tell me what in tarnation is so important?" he asked, a second before he glanced down to see an open smaller box within the large one. The box contained clippings from newspapers and magazines.

"Heiress Gone Missing" was written on

one headline. The rest were similar. Some said foul play was suspected.

When York spotted a photo splashed over the page of a newspaper, his chest thundered with excitement, but he wasn't sure why. He didn't know the woman in the photo, yet she was stunning. The most beautiful woman he'd ever laid eyes upon.

Huge eyes were framed by thick dark lashes, nestled in a heart-shaped face. The woman's pale skin didn't look like it had seen sunlight ever, and if he had to guess, she didn't tan. Her jet-black hair was tousled with a streak of color in it but since the photo was in black and white, he wasn't sure what color it was. She wore a black turtleneck and had on dark lipstick. Basically, she was the exact opposite of the women he usually found attractive. The types who thought the bigger the hair, the closer to God, and the ones who looked as if they had just stepped off the runway of a beauty pageant.

This woman looked deep. Like she had a secret no one else knew and an inner river that raged with thoughts, passion, and emotion.

The clipping was dated back thirty years.

"She's beautiful," whispered York.

"The picture doesn't really do her justice," said Petey, still rocking in place.

York's attention snapped to the man. "You knew her?"

Petey stared blankly at him. "You been hitting some of that moonshine Old Man McCreedy makes out in the forest?"

Baffled, York glanced to his brother. "What is he talking about?"

Louis nudged York's shoulder. "Read it."

York did—and then tensed. "Daughter of socialites Barton and Muffy Dumont has been missing for two months and if the rumors are to be believed, she's dead. Morgan Dumont was last seen... Hold up. Morgan, as in *our* Morgan?"

"Boy ain't the sharpest tool in the tool-shed, is he?" asked Petey, looking to Louis. "You suck up all them brain cells in the womb?"

York ignored the dig and fixated on the

photograph of Morgan. She was even more attractive than he'd imagined. Far more.

He wasn't sure how long he'd run his thumb over the picture of her before he realized his brother and Petey were staring at him. He cleared his throat and came back to his senses. "She's an heiress?"

Louis pulled out other clippings. "Not just any. Look."

Several of them showed photos of Morgan's grieving parents sitting on a sofa in their home being interviewed about the disappearance of their daughter. Morgan's mother had a poodle on her lap that was baring its teeth at the photographer. It took York a minute to realize what Louis was trying to point out to him.

In the background of the photos were items sitting on a side table. Having been raised around magical artifacts, and being a trained hunter, York knew demonic knick-knacks when he saw them, and he knew the telltale signs of the Collective. "No! She's not part of that! She can't be!"

"I don't know what to make of it all. We should ask her," said Louis, tapping the photo. "Her family is part of the Collective. Think Luc knows?"

"Of course not!" shouted York as he stood quickly. "No way would he permit her to be around if he knew she was working for the enemy."

"Hold up there," said Petey, waving a hand in the air. "I don't think she is. She's a good girl."

"Petey, that clock you see in the background on the table? It's one given to the highest-ranking members of the Collective. Think of it as a prize for being incredibly loyal," said Louis, shaking his head. "I can't believe she's been lying to us all these years. We trusted her. Why would she help us as children to stand against the Collective, and why help Virginia eight months ago?"

York thought back to when his sister had nearly been taken by a high-ranking Collective member. Morgan had fought the man, helping to protect Virginia until help could arrive. It didn't make sense.

His stomach dropped. "Dead Rising Day is almost here, and Daddy said Luc is missing some item that can bring the dead back to life. What if Morgan has been leading us all on for years, making us trust her, all so she could get her hands on whatever item Luc has and use Dead Rising Day to come back to life for good?"

"You're saying she's been playing a long con on everyone?" asked Petey, shaking his head. "No way. She's my friend. I trust her."

York couldn't stop the irrational mix of emotions that welled in him. Confusion. Betrayal. Lust. They swirled around deep in his gut before bubbling up and over. His anger won out. "I don't. She hasn't shown herself to me once in all these years. Why? Because she had something to hide?"

"We're getting ahead of ourselves here," said Louis, rising to his feet, holding the box of clippings. "We should talk with Luc about what we found."

"Darn straight," roared York. His response was a knee-jerk one. His shark side pushed upward quickly, clouding his better judgment. "He has a right to know she's been taking advantage of him for years, and I don't want to think of what she's capable of. Louis, where is the ghost extermination kit Daddy used to keep here?"

As the words left his mouth, he wanted them back. He was overreacting in a big way, and he knew it, yet as irrational as it was, he couldn't stop himself. His emotions were all over the place when it came to her.

There was a loud thump from just outside of the open door to the vault. A quick glance in that direction showed no one was there, and York's temper was too riled to focus on much beyond the possibility that Morgan had been playing them all for fools for years.

Petey gasped and shot forward. "Ain't nobody ghost-busting my friend. Any streams get crossed and you'll have me to deal with."

Louis moved toward York, the box still in his hands. "Calm down. You're taking this very personally."

Yes. Because it *was* personal. He felt something for her. A whole lot of some-things, and all along she'd been toying with them—with *him*.

Louis worked the clippings and informa-

MANDY M. ROTH

tion from York's grip and gave him a stern look. "This is one of those times Momma would tell you that you're putting the cart before the horse. We don't have the facts. We don't know the truth of the matter. Stop inventing one. You'll feel like a fool if you're wrong."

Petey gave York the stink eye. "And have a whole lot of crow to eat with Morgan if she finds out you were running your mouth the way you were. That girl ain't done nothing but look out for you and yours for years. She's given you no reason to stop trusting. Shame on you, New York."

It took some doing, but York's hurt and anger over the discovery that Morgan had connections to the Collective began to wane. He exhaled a shaky breath. "Why didn't she tell us her family is part of the Collective?"

Petey rolled his eyes. "That something you'd want on a billboard if your family was part of it?"

No.

York wouldn't want anyone to know he was related to evil zealots. He shook his head.

Petey grunted again. "Got more brawn than brain."

Louis snorted. "Yes. He does."

"You look just like me," warned York.

Louis smirked. "But I'm smart enough to know not to think the absolute worst about someone we call a friend."

York took a moment to really soak in the number of boxes before them. It had to be an entire wardrobe there, not to mention countless personal items. "Where did this all come from?"

"It was on the morning delivery truck," said Louis, setting down the clippings and picking up a small black handbag. He opened it and withdrew the small billfold within. "I don't think any of this has been touched since she went missing."

"You mean died," corrected Petey. "She wasn't missing. She was dead. We know that now."

York's throat constricted. "D-does it say anywhere how she died or where they found her body?"

His brother locked gazes with him. "That's just it. From what I was reading through here, they never did find her body. She was finally declared dead years after she went missing. And if I'm reading this all right, her parents insisted the search for her be called off far sooner than the authorities wanted to. But they had friends in high places, so they got what they wanted."

"You're joking, right?" demanded York, his ire rising again but this time over Morgan's parents. They didn't want their daughter found? What kind of parents were they?

"There you are," said Luc, appearing in the doorway. He glanced around, his brows drawing together at the sight of the boxes. "What's going on? How did you get all of this?"

"Arrived this morning," said Louis, shoving the billfold at York, who absently put it in his back pocket as Luc hurried into the room with them.

"This was all at my New York brownstone," said Luc as he bent and lifted a black teddy bear from one of the boxes. "None of this should be here."

"Why did you have it all?" asked Louis. "Were you storing it for Morgan?"

Luc lowered his gaze, his shoulders slumping. "She doesn't know I have it. I did my best to keep the fact her parents had her belongings packed within three days of her death from her."

Petey propped an elbow on one of the many shelving units in the vault, the one where the crystal balls were stored. Every hunter's relic facility had a similar section. "So the minute they finally had her declared dead and gone, they boxed up all her stuff?"

It was hard to miss the sorrow in the old man's voice.

Luc stood slowly. "No. I mean three days after they gave her as an offering to the Collective, to be killed and have her soul captured, they boxed up everything that reminded them of her and put it out at the curb for trash pickup. I saw to it that it was all stored somewhere safe."

York mulled over everything he'd just heard and clenched his fists. "They gave her to the Collective as a sacrifice?"

"Yes," said Luc evenly. "And before you

think the worst of her, Morgan had no idea her family was part of the Collective. She didn't know anything about the supernatural until she died, and I opened her eyes to it all. Before that, she was just the only child of wealthy absentee parents who cared more about money and power than they did their daughter."

Louis and Petey both set their attention on York.

His face heated. He'd done just as Petey had claimed. He'd thought the worst of her without knowing the whole truth.

Chapter Six

"LOUIS?" called out Morgan as she stood inside Enchanted Collectibles & Antiques. The shop had large front windows to showcase its offerings with hand-painted lettering on them, announcing the store's hours. The displays set up in the windows changed often. Currently, they were dedicated to vintage medical equipment. To Morgan, it mostly looked macabre and like torture devices.

Curiosity got the better of her, and she went toward a collection of antique prosthetics. Next to the limbs were three anatomically correct dolls carved from wood that looked a lot like they were set up for an autopsy. She understood they'd been used in a teaching capacity, or at least that was what she hoped.

She lifted out the carved intestines of one of the dolls and held it up, wondering who would want to own something like that. Then she remembered where she was: Hedgewitch Cove. The grotesque item would have a home before long. If Betty saw them, she'd want the collection of dolls for herself.

"To each their own," she said with a shake of her head before continuing her quest to locate Louis. She popped in and out of the multitude of rooms in the main portion of the shop. There was no sign of Louis or Leo. That was strange. They didn't generally leave the store open and unattended.

Morgan reappeared in the main section of the shop, near the front windows, and glanced out, spotting York's truck in a parking space. Obviously, they were here, which meant they were more than likely downstairs in the vault area.

She headed for the back stairs and the

minute she began her descent, she heard voices. At first, they were muffled—but when they became clear, she froze on the stairs, unable to believe her ears.

"Dead Rising Day is almost here, and Daddy said Luc is missing some item that can bring the dead back to life. What if Morgan has been leading us all on for years, making us trust her, all so she could get her hands on whatever item Luc has and use Dead Rising Day to come back to life for good?" asked York, his deep voice booming through the hall.

His words pierced her heart. Why would he think she was leading them on or that she had designs on Dead Rising Day?

"You're saying she's been playing a long con on everyone?" Petey asked, and it was easy to hear he didn't agree with whatever the topic was. "No way. She's my friend. I trust her."

At least Petey had her back.

"I don't," snapped York.

Morgan leaned against the wall of the staircase and tried to keep from crying. It didn't work.

He kept saying horrible things about her. Things that were simply untrue.

The shouting continued, and the second she heard York demanding to know where the ghost extermination kit was, she was in a full-blown emotional meltdown, sobbing silently as she shook her head, unsure what had prompted the rage coming from York.

The overpowering need to be anywhere other than near York hit her hard. From the mix of tears, frustration, and bewilderment, she didn't stop to think of merely popping away and back to the inn. She used a mode of transportation she rarely used in death.

Her legs.

Morgan turned so fast that she thumped the wall and tripped up the stairs in her urge to escape the scrutiny she was being subjected to. She made it to the main level of the shop but was in such a blind panic that she didn't pay attention to where she was going. She just ran, and ended up crashing into one of the front displays. In the next breath, she found herself on the floor of the shop in a mass of wooden body parts, creepy dolls, and other artifacts, all strewn around her.

Morgan rolled onto her side, and something jabbed her in the knee. Without thought, she reached down—and found the exact box that Luc had sent her to the shop to ask about. It was popped open, with shiny gold coins spilling out of it.

Not just any coins either.

No.

Ones she'd seen a version of before.

They looked just like the enchanted coins from Blackbeard's treasure. The coins that had been swept up in Marie-Claire Caillat's spell to help her grandchildren find their mates. The coins that were, in effect, cursed.

Did that mean it was Louis's turn to find his mate? That the curse had selected him as the next Peugeot destined to cross paths with their chosen one—the person they'd end up spending their lives with?

It made sense. After all, Louis ran the shop.

As she focused on the box, the one Luc had been anxious to find, she couldn't stop the urge to make contact with it. Her fingers slid over the wood and to the burned-in symbols of crescent moons, stars, and a pentagram.

Her mind raced, and it struck her then that she'd seen that very combination of symbols before when she'd been alive. It had been on a few small items her father had in his home office, along with a clock that sat on the table behind the sofa in the formal living room of her parents' home.

What did the symbol mean, and why did they have it on things?

Moreover, what did Luc want with it now? And what did it all have to do with Louis and his mate?

Absently, she lifted a gold coin while still lying on the floor of the shop. As her fingers connected with the coin, they heated. Something that hadn't happened since she'd been dead.

With a gasp, she dropped the coin and it landed in a way that showed the same symbol that was carved into the top of the box. The compulsion to touch the coin again hit her with such a force that denying it wasn't possible.

She flipped the coin over, feeling the same warmth as before, and couldn't rip her gaze from what was on the other side of the coin.

It was the outline of the state of New York, along with an embossed outline of the statue of liberty.

Her breath caught.

The curse had selected York? It was his turn to find his special someone?

As much as she wanted to be happy for him, it was impossible not to feel a pang of jealousy. She wasn't sure why it happened. The man thought she was working for the enemy. That she was part of the Collective. Why on earth should she care if he found his mate or not?

"Oh, there you are, dear," said Betty, suddenly standing near Morgan in the center of the shop.

The older woman hadn't been there only a second prior, and Morgan had never heard the door to the shop ding to indicate someone was entering. As far as Morgan knew, Betty didn't possess the ability to vanish and reappear out of thin air, much like Morgan could do.

Yet, there she was, plain as day.

Morgan pushed to her feet slowly, doing her best not to fall over all of the mess she'd made. "Betty, I thought you were napping. What are you doing over here?"

"I followed Luc," she said, standing perfectly still, the slightest of smiles touching her lips.

"Luc is here? I didn't pass him," Morgan stated, feeling a bit like she'd fallen down a rabbit hole.

"Because it's begun," returned Betty, as if that explained everything. She held out her hand to Morgan. In it was the brooch she cherished. "Take this, dear. You'll need it for safe passage."

"Safe passage?" questioned Morgan, reaching out and taking the brooch.

Betty's grin widened as another coin appeared out of thin air next to the older woman. She snatched it with cat-like reflexes, plunking it down into Morgan's palm with the brooch. As she did, the pin of the brooch stuck Morgan's palm. It hurt, which surprised Morgan.

What shocked her even more was the sight of blood pooling on her palm.

She was a ghost.

She didn't bleed.

"Betty?"

Before she could ask any more questions, the room began to swirl at a rapid rate. Dizzy and disoriented, Morgan stumbled and tripped over the mess on the floor once again. But when she fell, the floor didn't catch her.

Nothing did.

She simply tumbled through blackness, her hand wrapped around the brooch and coin for dear life. Something slammed into her, feeling as if it was moving through her, or rather, she was moving through it. The next she knew, she struck something hard and stopped moving.

Morgan groaned and opened her eyes to find herself staring up at the underside of an old rusty fire escape that was hooked to a brick building. Graffiti covered the brick, and it instantly reminded her of the '80s and the tagging art that she used to see in various areas of New York.

As she took a deep breath in and smelled garbage and Chinese takeout, she couldn't help but instantly feel a pang and longing for home—the city she'd not been in since her death.

Moreover, she felt positive she was not in Hedgewitch Cove any longer.

Disoriented, Morgan propped herself up on her elbows, wondering where she was and how she'd gotten there. A quick glance down at herself revealed that her clothing had changed. What she was currently in wasn't something from her closet.

In fact, she'd not seen the outfit in thirty years.

Since the night of her death.

Why was she dressed in what she'd been wearing when she died? Had the rules of the afterlife up and changed on her all of a sudden? Would she be stuck in a mini-skirt and shirt that announced her love of New York?

She really hoped not.

She pushed the brooch and the coin into the small pocket in her skirt for safekeeping.

Her weird meter had undoubtedly changed significantly since her passing and afterlife in Hedgewitch Cove. She'd gone from knowing nothing of the supernatural to considering herself something of an expert on the subject matter. But even she had to admit, this was up there with the top ten weird things that had ever happened to her.

"Where am I?" she asked, hoping the answer would come to her.

It didn't.

She realized she was in an alley of a large city. As she glanced sideways, she saw cars at the end of the alley, out on the street, going by, as well as people walking.

At first, she couldn't put her finger on what was off, aside from the obvious, which was not being in Hedgewitch Cove any longer. That wasn't exactly strange. Not with what her not-so-alive life had become. But there was certainly something that wasn't right with the scene before her.

When she looked harder and really took note of not only the vehicles she was seeing but the clothing everyone had on, a sinking feeling came over her. Reaching up, she rubbed her eyes, positive they were deceiving her.

Surely she wasn't seeing all the shoulder-pad-loving outfits she thought she was seeing. And what was with all the parachute pants? Had there been a run on vintage clothing that she'd not been alerted to?

A loose flyer blew down the alley at her, and she caught it quickly. As she flipped it over and read it, her breath caught.

It was an announcement for the very concert she'd died at thirty years prior.

Every clue around her that she wasn't in the time she'd started in struck her at once, and she scrambled to her feet. She ran in the direction of people, expecting to go unnoticed by them as was always the case unless she was actively showing herself.

When she collided with a man in pegged jeans, slide-on tennis shoes, a yellow shirt, and a sweatshirt tied over his shoulders, she jerked back. He stopped talking on his over-size cell phone and lowered his Ray-Bans to look her up and down. He then grinned in a way that said he was fine with being run into by her, and that he could most certainly see her.

"Sorry," she said fast, her pulse racing as she took off in a run down the street. "Luc!"

He didn't respond, and she didn't stop running until she spotted a newspaper stand.

She launched herself at the papers, desperate to know the date. When she saw it, she fought the urge to be sick. "No. It can't be."

"Can't be what?" asked the man in a leather cap who was running the stand.

She pointed to the front of the paper. "Is this date right?"

The man stared at her a second and then sighed. "Drugs. Messes with your mind. Of course it's the right day. What other day would it be?"

Part of her hoped she'd figure out she was dreaming and not really back in time.

In the very year and day that she'd died.

Chapter Seven

THERE WAS A COMMOTION FROM UPSTAIRS, and within seconds Betty was at the doorway to the vault. She stopped just shy of entering, looking as sweet and demure as ever. She stared in at the boxes and then at York. "Why are you here? You should already be there."

Luc sighed. "Betty, you should be at the inn. Bob was supposed to be keeping an eye on you."

"If I'm there, I can't be here, sweet boy," she said to the devil, as if she were his grandmother and he wasn't the guy in charge of all evil.

The strangest feeling that Morgan was present struck him hard.

"Morgan!" shouted York, hoping she was in the area and would reply.

She didn't.

He tried two more times before yanking his phone from his pocket, his intent to call the inn to speak to her.

Betty laughed. "You're going to need a very good coverage plan to reach her where she is now."

His stomach dropped. "Where she is now?"

Petey stepped up closer to him. "Betty, where exactly is Morgan? She didn't go into no light, did she? Remember when Carol Ann did that? Was all the rage too when that Hollywood guy heard about her. Went and made a movie about her. Don't know why they had that actress girl getting sucked into a television. We all know it was a radio. Remember when everyone in town could only get the same station? The one with children's songs playing? That's what happens when kids get sucked into radio airwaves by the supernatural."

York had heard mention of the incident several times in the past, but it predated him and it wasn't his primary concern at the moment. Morgan was. "Betty, do you know where Morgan is?"

She nodded but said nothing.

"Well?" demanded York, earning him a hard grunt from Luc.

Luc went to Betty, taking a different approach with her. "Betty, did you see Morgan?"

"I did," said Betty, pride in her voice. "She was upstairs, running like a banshee from down this way. Have you ever seen a banshee run? It's quite a sight, especially since they don't have feet. What was Morgan running from? Was it Christmas music? That will be starting before you know it. Downright terrifying if you ask me. All that jingling, merriment, and good cheer."

She shuddered.

"Thank the hellions, Howie isn't around to hear it. That boy has a real fear of Jolly Old Saint Nick. I offered to eat Santa. I'm sure he's delicious with all those extra pounds and being stuffed full of cookies. But, alas, do-gooders give me indigestion."

Luc cleared his throat. "Focus for me, Betty. Morgan was just here in the shop?"

"Oh yes. She was. I think she might have heard all the fuss about her," said Betty, sliding her gaze toward York. "Heard that you don't trust her. That you think she's with the Collective. That wasn't very nice, York. You should really tell her you're sorry. If you don't, I might get the urge to bake you a pie. You wouldn't want that, would you?"

Louis laughed and partially covered it with a cough. "Shark pie. It will be a hot seller at the local bake sale."

York sighed. "No, I wouldn't like that. Betty, I opened my mouth and inserted my foot. I don't think she's the enemy. I just...it's just..."

"She's your mate and confuses you?" asked Betty.

"Yes," replied York, before shaking his head fast. "No. I mean, she's just...I don't know."

Louis gasped. "Brother, your gut reaction to Betty's question was yes, Morgan is your mate. Is that true? Is Morgan your special someone?"

"She's dead," said York, understanding that meant she couldn't be his mate. That his mate would be alive. "She can't be mine."

"But you wish she was," said Louis, earning him a hard glare from York, who wanted the topic to end. He wasn't the type to lay his feelings out on the line in front of others. At least not feelings that left him vulnerable. And the way he felt for Morgan certainly did just that. He felt stripped bare when it came to her, and knowing he'd upset her the way he had was like pouring salt in a wound.

Had he just kept his temper in check and his mouth shut, all would be fine. Now he had to hunt her down and find a way back into her good graces. Did the woman even have those when it came to him? He wasn't sure. She mostly seemed annoyed by his very presence. Not that he could blame her. He *was* on the annoying side.

Luc crossed his arms over his chest, his chin out, his shoulders back as he surveyed

York. "Well? Do you want her to be your special someone or not?"

"He gets a choice?" asked Petey, making himself known in the conversation once more. "I didn't know we got choices."

"You don't," snapped Luc, his irritation clearly with York, not Petey. "The choice is made for each of you long before you ever come to be. I just want to hear what York has to say on the matter."

Petey bit at his lower lip. "I can't tell if you're rooting for him to want it or for him *not* to want it. I'm confused."

Betty smiled sweetly. "Join the club, dear. I'm always confused anymore."

Luc's gaze narrowed on York. "I don't know which I'm hoping for. Part of me wants to snap York in half for daring to have feelings for Morgan. Though it's not exactly a shock to me. Still, I don't know that I like it."

"I don't have…well…I might have some small feelings for her," corrected York before defeat set in. "Okay. More than a small amount."

Luc made a move to come at him, but

Betty was quick to step in the devil's path, putting up her small hand, halting Luc's progress instantly. "Now, now. No eating him. If I'm not allowed to, neither can you. Fair is fair."

"I don't eat people," said Luc firmly. "Normally. Though I would be willing to make an exception. I could grow to like the taste of marine life. I'm sure."

Petey tipped his head in York's direction. "Way to go. You stepped in it with the devil. Even I got more sense than that."

"Just how much more than a small amount are we talking about here," demanded Luc about York's feelings for Morgan.

York stared down at the fallen newspaper clippings with Morgan's photo on them. He opened his mouth to lie about not wanting her, but the truth popped out. "I want her more than I've ever wanted anything. Mostly though, I want her to know how sorry I am for what I said. For thinking the worst of her. I don't know why she's never showed herself to me, but that doesn't matter. What matters is she knows I do trust her. That I'm sorry."

"Don't be silly, New York," said Betty sternly. "The poor child hasn't shown herself to you because deep down, a part of her knew the two of you are connected. Wouldn't have done her a lot of good to have you looking at her with stars in your eyes when you were just a boy. She had to wait until you were a grown man. And then she had to wait until the time was right. When that time came, I think she felt the urge but denied it, worried because she's not like the women you traipse around with. She's better. Much better."

York just stood there, his mouth partially open as if he were catching flies, as he took his verbal scolding from a woman who frequently seemed out of her mind but currently sounded as though she knew exactly what she was talking about.

Louis grinned. "She's not wrong."

Luc nodded. "True. Betty, where is Morgan?"

"You mean when, dear," said Betty, making Luc's entire body stiffen.

York caught the response and worry

slashed through him. "What does she mean by when?"

Luc's gaze narrowed on Betty. "They were to go back together. York was supposed to be with her, to help her find the contract her parents signed, and then be what tethers her to time—to the here and now—to his rightful time. Tell me she's not in the past, alone."

York had heard and seen a lot of weird things in his life. So much so that not many things made him take pause. But this did. "What? Are you telling me she time-traveled into the past? That's not possible."

Louis put a hand up, and then with his other hand, he pointed at Luc, pretending to block the motion. "Pretty sure the devil can time jump with ease. Guessing it's very possible."

"I can see and hear you," said Luc with an annoyed huff.

York didn't have time for the level of crazy Hedgewitch Cove residents tended to bring to every situation. He needed to find Morgan, and fast. He darted around Betty and raced up the stairs to the main room, only to find it in shambles. The shark in him instantly took note of the scent of blood and his mouth burned with the need to shift shapes.

The mess hadn't been here only minutes prior. If Morgan had been up here, what had happened to her? Had someone attacked her?

Louis ran into him from behind, nearly knocking him over. "What happened up here?"

"Morgan!" shouted York through the beginning of a shifting mouth. "Something is wrong."

"Nonsense," said Betty, meandering up alongside the men as if she didn't have a care in the world. "Something is right. She's gone back to where it began."

Luc was suddenly there as well. "She traveled back to the day she died?"

Betty nodded.

Luc paled. "As I said, York was supposed to be with her. I saw him years ago. He's the one who kills some of the Collective members sent to steal her soul. If she's there, alone, they'll win. They'll take her soul. One

I've kept guarded for decades from them. This is playing out all wrong!"

Betty patted the man's forearm. "No. It's playing out as it should. She has my brooch."

Luc closed his eyes and hung his head in defeat. "We're going to lose her to the enemy. They'll whisk her soul off to a location even I can't get to, and her body, which I've kept in a mystical stasis, will rot and die. Her soul and her body are still mystically linked. One can't be without the other. It's part of the price to be paid for what I did."

Louis shot a hand in the air. "Her *what* that you did *what* with?"

Petey entered the main area of the shop. He took a look at the items on the floor and let out a low, long whistle. "It's been raining fake body parts in here. Better than that one freak storm we got around here when it rained real body parts."

"Says you," corrected Betty. "That was one of my favorite days. I really wish my sisters had been here for it. Leva-Joyce could have made her famous beans with leg calves and Mildred could have done her biscuits and blood gravy. Oh, I'm hungry just thinking about all the wonderful dishes we could have made together."

York dismissed Betty's ramblings and focused in on the mess on the floor, where he continued to smell blood. He pushed through the wooden body parts and bent, his finger connecting with a small drop of crimson on the floor. The second the red liquid made contact with his skin, his finger heated, and his senses went into overdrive. "It's blood."

"From how worked up you're getting, I'm going to assume that is Morgan's blood," said Petey.

"Ghosts bleed?" asked Louis, stealing York's very words.

Luc bent near York, and the forlorn look on the devil's face worried him. "She's not a ghost, per se."

York's body tensed. "Then what, exactly, is she?"

Swallowing hard, Luc met his gaze. "My goddaughter. A person I've viewed as a daughter all of her life, and someone I knew from the first breath she took was created for someone important to me. That person was you. I've struggled with that knowledge for years. See, I may be the devil, but Morgan is special to me. I'd rather she join a convent than have any man touch her. So, while I like you, I pretty much want to smite you because you're male and into her. And yes, I know you weren't born yet back when all this first went down, but I'm in touch with things on a level I can't explain in words to you.

"I knew from day one she was, is, important. That she helps tip the scale of good and evil. And I did all I could to talk her parents out of signing a contract for her soul. They wouldn't listen, and I'm only allowed to interfere to a point, then anything I do is undone but with worse consequences. It's the laws of nature, and even I can only bend them so far without them breaking."

York opened his mouth to question Luc, but the devil kept ranting.

"When I learned she'd been marked by a powerful master vampire for conversion because of who her parents were, I stepped in then. The vampire sent one of his top men after Morgan, unbeknownst to her. I turned that vampire into a bat, and then gave it to her as a pet; its penance was having to always protect her. I did the same thing to the first demon who came for her, when she was in her teens. Turned him into a hedgehog though. Same deal. He had to protect her. And they did. I thought I'd solved all the problems. Then I got her tickets to a concert for her birthday, and was called away for work when I felt it—her death."

Chapter Eight

LOUIS AND YORK shared dual shocked expressions.

"You're Morgan's godfather?" asked York.

Luc nodded.

Petey put his hand up slightly. "I knew that. She confessed it to me during one of our late-night talks. She was trying to help me fight off the urge to shift and run in the full moon. I'm not as young as I used to be. Shifting fully can take it out of me. She's a good girl. Doesn't know she's not a ghost though.

"When Betty told me you'd hidden Morgan's human body in a secure room in hell, where no one would think to look or bother it, where it wouldn't age but could heal slowly, and that you brought Morgan's soul here to Hedgewitch Cove, knowing the town's spells would protect it from detection by the Collective, I understood the evil genius side of your reputation. Then I saw you turn your nose up at a ham sandwich with potato chips, ketchup, and hot sauce, and began to rethink it all. Ain't nobody with a lick of sense gonna turn their noses up at that sandwich. It's delicious."

Morgan's body was hidden away? This was news to York. He'd always just assumed she was a ghost with no body tucked safely away. Once, he'd come close to asking Luc what cemetery Morgan had been buried in because he wanted to go to it and be sure the site was tended to. Ultimately, he'd been unable to bring himself to ask the question, worried that seeing a headstone with her name on it would toy with his mind too much.

All this time he'd been unable to come face-to-face with the reality that she was dead and gone, and she wasn't?

York stood quickly, his mind racing. "So, she's not dead?"

"She's not," said Luc.

"And you have her body somewhere?" asked York.

Luc nodded. "I do. It's safe. It's in the only place I could think that no one would enter in hell."

"The laundry room? I hate doing laundry," said Petey.

Luc rolled his eyes. "No. The chapel."

"Hell has a church?" questioned Louis.

"Not the point here, brother," warned York. "The point is, Morgan isn't dead, and Luc has her body tucked away."

"Maybe. Maybe not," said Betty.

Luc rose as well, his gaze sweeping to Betty. Surprise was etched on the man's face. "You swore to keep the secret always."

Betty began to rock back and forth and hum a merry tune before bending and lifting one of the haunted dolls that had been on display in the front window. The doll held an eerie resemblance to the photo of Morgan with dark hair, big eyes, and pale skin. Betty smoothed the doll's dress and righted its hair in a loving manner. "Who's a pretty little demonic spirit attached to this dolly? That's right. You are."

Louis cleared his throat. "I'm sorry, but did you say that doll has a demon attached to it?"

Luc shook his head. "Not anymore. It used to years ago but it's long since moved on to an item a child was more likely to play with in today's day and age."

"One of them gaming boxes?" asked Petey, giving the doll the side-eye as if he didn't quite believe there wasn't anything demonic about it any longer.

The doll's eyes, which were made to open and close, popped open fully, and Petey leaped back so fast he hit another display unit. This one had glass bottles with various scenes built in them. Some had what looked like tiny fairy mounds and others had old-time pirate ships in them.

The ship ones reminded York greatly of the ship in the bottle that Blackbeard had. Years ago, York had organized a prank that left the pirate trapped in his bottle for some time. While York had found the entire ordeal comical, Blackbeard had not, and since he wasn't your average, run-of-the-mill ghost and had a lot of natural-born magic in him, making him angry had been very foolish.

Louis hurried over to the bottles and began inspecting them, shaking his head in a disapproving manner at Petey as he did. "You're lucky you didn't break any. Two of them are portals to other magical realms."

"Shouldn't that be locked away in a vault or something?" asked Petey, dropping a bottle that he'd only just picked up.

Groaning, Louis removed the item from Petey's reach and checked it over carefully. "They don't play well near the other relics. And all signs pointed to me needing to go ahead and set some out on display. Guess Fate has something in store for them."

"Here's to hoping it's not the apocalypse," said Petey before he reached out and touched one of the bottles that hadn't fallen from the shelf. He lifted it and shook it, as if it were a snow globe. The scene was one depicting a small log cabin on a mountainside in a heavily wooded area. Leaves on the tiny ornate trees began to fall all over within the bottle, much like snowflakes would in a snow globe. "But that would make Arnold happy. Maybe we should break one just to give him a sporting chance at the end he's been counting on."

Luc and Louis were quick to disarm the crazy old man of the bottle before he actually did trigger the end of days. It would be a very Petey thing to do.

Louis was first to the item, and he held it close to his chest protectively. "I'll need to call out to Old Man McCreedy's place in the Blue Ridge Mountains. He's going to wonder why he just had a freak earthquake with high winds."

Petey lifted a bushy brow. "That one is tied to that old fart's place? Give it back. I'm gonna shake it some more."

Betty was still lovingly tending to the formerly possessed doll. She even kissed its forehead. "Protect her always. Never let the bad near her," whispered Betty in her singsong voice. "Get her back to the start and to her mate before Dead Rising Day, when the magic of the day can hide the devil's magic from others."

Everyone stopped and stared at her.

She continued on, "Got to hide the flux of power from the others who won't understand. Have to make the union of the body and the soul look like it's a by-product of Dead Rising Day. Not because the devil willed it so."

Louis, who was still cradling Old Man McCreedy's place, blinked several times. "I'm a little rusty on my Betty translations so I'm unclear if she's talking about something made up, something from long ago, or maybe Morgan."

"Two out of three isn't so bad, dear," said Betty, her attention still on the doll.

Luc let out on a long, semi-annoyed breath. "Betty, we discussed this before. I was very clear on what you could and could not reveal about Morgan's situation."

"What situation?" demanded York, suddenly feeling as if he were wound tighter than a corkscrew.

Betty's gaze snapped to him. "Child, Luc swore to me you're a bright boy. There are days I wonder if his rose-colored glasses for your family cloud his judgment."

"Did she just call me dim-witted?" asked York.

"I do it all the time. Why should she be different?" Louis shrugged, lost his grip on the bottle, and dropped it. The bottle hit the ground and several trees fell over in it, just missing the log cabin.

Petey laughed long and hard. "Serves that old goat right. He cheats at poker and he fibs about the size of his catch when fishing."

"You're still upset he took a shot at you while you were in wolf form on his property," said Luc, pulling Petey back from the bottle a second before Petey's foot would have not-so-accidentally connected with it.

Petey stepped back from Luc and rubbed his backside. "You ever try picking buckshot out of your butt? Ain't fun at all."

Louis managed to get the bottle to the counter of the shop without further incident. "I'm going to need to talk to Virginia about baking McCreedy some pies for me to send out. Seems only right since I nearly leveled his house with trees. I still can't believe he crossed the coven close to him to the point they cursed his land and tied its fate to this bottle. Even worse, if the bottle gets too close to the property, it *and* the property go boom."

"Cross?" said Petey with a snort. "Try was engaged to be married to the head of the coven long ago and started stepping out on her with another witch. You don't cheat on a witch. Trust me. I didn't, but someone lied to my sweetie and told her otherwise, and I've been paying the price for that for a very long time. I'm like an expert on just how vengeful a witchy woman can be."

Everyone nodded, including Betty.

Petey certainly would know. At one point, he and York's grandmother had been an item. York didn't know the specifics of what had gone down, but he did know lies had been told to his grandmother and her temper had gotten the better of her tongue. She'd inadvertently cursed the man. Petey'd had that black cloud over him ever since.

There was a spark between his grandmother and Petey still to this day, and they'd been spending more and more time together. York didn't know where it all might lead, but he did hope his grandmother would find happiness. And she could do far worse than Petey. The man's heart was pure—even if he did want to kick Old Man McCreedy's cursed bottle.

York had met McCreedy once when they'd needed to go to North Carolina to take a magical relic to the hunters there. McCreedy was a character all unto himself. Cranky and about as mountain as could be. He was country through and through. Not that York had a lot of room to talk.

Betty stared up at Luc. "I'm going to miss Morgan when she's gone."

York lurched forward. "Gone? To where? What do you mean?"

Sadness touched her face. "She won't live with us anymore. Luc said so. When the body and soul unite."

"Someone needs to tell me what, exactly, is going on with Morgan," he snapped.

Petey pulled out a fishing lure from his pocket and began to clean under his finger-nails with it. "Why? You think she's the enemy."

"Do not," said York.

"Do so," argued Petey.

Luc groaned. "Enough."

Petey put the lure back in his pocket while sticking his tongue out at York. "Do so."

The man got the last word on the topic.

Luc gently put a hand on Betty's shoulder. "You've been very talkative about Morgan and her situation. While I know you sometimes get a little confused lately, I also know you well enough to know you'd never put Morgan at risk. You love her. She's been an important part of your journey of learning to value human life."

Nodding, Betty went back to centering her attention on the doll. "She was so tiny when I first met her. Looked like such a tasty morsel. Millie said I couldn't eat her. That she wasn't a snack. She was a sweet, sweet baby that was important to the devil. A baby we were to protect."

"Millie?" asked Louis, before York could think to do so.

Petey leaned and spoke out of the side of his mouth as if spilling a grand secret. "Millie is Mildred. One of Betty's sisters."

"Mildred knew Morgan as a baby?" asked York. "Why didn't Morgan mention that before?"

"She don't know it. Millie doesn't live here and hasn't come to visit Betty since Morgan came to be here in town," said Petey, still doing the world's worst version of whispering. "Been waiting for the right time."

Betty nodded. "The time is just about here. Millie is on her way. Should be here before we know it. I just hope Morgan doesn't get killed—again. I should have made sure York was with her when I reunited her with her body. He could have kept her safer."

Luc gasped. "Her body isn't in the chapel anymore?"

Betty hugged the doll tighter. "No. She has it. She's in it. Not like the skin suits some demons wear, but as herself. I don't think she'd have picked it if given a chance. I mean, it is human after all and humans only have two eyes. How do they see behind them with only two eyes and heads that don't swivel all the way around?" She clutched the doll tighter. "My skin suit itches."

The men shared a look that said they didn't want to know more about Betty and her skin suit.

York's magic—which wasn't his go-to response to anything, as he took after his father more than his mother, who hailed from a long line of powerful witches— decided to pick then to make itself known. It buzzed and then beat at him from within, as if it were a caged animal on the verge of breaking free.

Now wasn't the time to lose it.

Morgan was on her own in the past, alive, and in danger. She wouldn't be getting another do-over. There would be no more saving her body in any special hiding place in hell. If she died again, she'd be the Collective's pawn, their prisoner for eternity.

His fingers began to tingle as he drew natural energy from the Earth. The power filled him, putting his shark on edge. He bristled with the overwhelming need to release the building magic, but doing so could and would be dangerous.

"C-call Momma and Mémé," he managed through clenched teeth as he shot his twin a look of desperation. The women would be able to get him under control. There was no telling what would happen if his magic was left unchecked. He could very well make Petey's tampering with the cursed bottle appear tame.

Louis ran for the antique phone he kept at the shop since he eschewed most of the amenities that modern times had brought about.

In the blink of an eye, Betty was there, yanking the phone from Louis's grip with one hand while she held the doll in the other. Her arm went up and up and up, stretching in a way that defied logic. By the time she was done, the phone was across the shop, while Betty remained near the counter with Louis. York wasn't sure which he should be more shocked by: the fact Betty's arm could do that or the proof of just how long the cord on his brother's phone was.

Betty's face showed nothing but tenderness. "No calls for help, dear. Let him blow."

"What?" asked Louis. "He could take out the entire state."

"And turn into York hamburger," offered Petey. "That will be hard to get out of the drapes."

"Nonsense," she returned.

Luc moved in to assist. He attempted to ease Betty back from Louis and get the phone receiver. Neither worked. Never a good sign when the devil couldn't control a demon. "Betty, Louis is right. York is a danger right now. Help is needed."

"All that is needed is for him to go to her," said Betty, standing her ground.

Petey sauntered over to the phone receiver and pried it gently from Betty's grip.

Her head whipped around and her gaze locked on him. She looked like a stone-cold predator. Not someone's great-grandmother.

Petey flashed a silly smile. "Don't go giving me that sass, woman. I ain't gonna let him call anyone. I understand what you're saying. I speak fluent bat-crazy. It's kind of my thing."

Betty nodded, obviously agreeing that Petey was nuts.

Petey nodded to York. "Let your magic do what feels right. She's trying to tell you that you have the power in you to get to your mate. Don't matter what time she's in. Let the magic lead you to her. I'd tell you not to overthink but I'm talking to you, not Louis, so there ain't much chance of that happening."

Had everyone gone plum crazy? Couldn't they all see how on edge he was?

As he began to panic more, his magic increased. It reached a level he'd never before felt and he spun fast, bending down in the fetal position, worried he'd explode with power and kill everyone around him. He didn't want anyone else hurt on account of him.

"Get the contract!" yelled Luc. "And remember there are two Morgan's back there now. The one of old and the one you've come to know. Save the Morgan of the now—of the future!"

There was a boom of sorts, but it wasn't the one he'd been expecting. When it cleared, there was only the slightest hint of remaining magic clinging to the air.

York stayed hunched over for a moment more, worried that he'd look up to find his friends and brother were no more. When he finally mustered the courage to open his eyes and lift his head, he found they were indeed gone—but so was everything that had been around him.

The shop was gone and as far as he could tell, so was Hedgewitch Cove. Tall buildings surrounded him now, as did a mass of people who barely paid any mind to him, despite the fact he was a six-and-a-half-foot-tall adult male bent over in the center of a busy sidewalk.

As he soaked in the sights around him, it clicked. Betty had been right. His magic had done the impossible. It had whisked him into the past. He was no expert on the '80s, but he felt secure enough to say he was standing in that decade.

He stood quickly, his body on the verge of a shift. His shark side wanted to locate Morgan as much as he did. It took him a second to calm himself enough to think rationally. When he did, he remembered having Morgan's billfold in his back pocket.

He withdrew it and looked at the address listed on the identification.

He then stepped out in front of a man in a business suit, who was on an obscenely large cellphone, his arm outstretched, with a hard-shell briefcase in his hand as he tried to hail a taxi.

The minute York stepped out and into the street, an oncoming taxi came to a dead stop. The man with the phone tried to get in but York growled, his shark side still there, just below the surface. Whatever the man saw made him think twice about pushing York.

Instead, the man nodded and stepped back. "It's all yours, buddy."

York got in and showed the identification to the driver and then pulled out his own wallet and withdrew a large bill. "Can you take me here?"

"I can, but I don't take funny money," said the man.

"Funny money?" asked York.

"That's no real hundred-dollar bill," said the cab driver.

It was.

York looked at the bill and realized it was a newer one-hundred-dollar bill. Something that wasn't in circulation in the '80s. To the driver, it probably did look a lot like money that came in a board game, not real. Quickly, York looked into Morgan's billfold and found more than enough money there. He pulled out a hundred from hers and held it up. "That work?"

"It does," said the man with a grin. "I'll break every law to get you there in record time for that."

"Good. See that you do. A life depends on it."

Chapter Nine

MORGAN WALKED at a brisk pace on the sidewalk, tears stinging her eyes as she tried and failed to make sense of what was happening to her. It began to drizzle, and she came to a sudden stop as the water brushed her skin. It was something she'd not felt in thirty years.

As much as she used to long to feel rain and heat and anything, having it all happen at once, without an understanding as to why, was too much. Everything she'd come to know as her reality had been turned upside down. A deep nagging told her this was serious. Life-or-death kind of serious, and since she'd been dead to start with, that was worrisome. As the light rain continued to sprinkle down upon her skin, she stopped long enough to take inventory of her situation.

The longer she stood in place, the more she knew without a shadow of a doubt that this wasn't the same existence she'd been living, for lack of a better word. This was different. This was like when she was alive. A sure sign she was right came when her stomach rumbled loudly. Hunger pains weren't something she'd experienced in thirty years.

She'd worry about eating later. For now, she needed to find a way back to the time she'd left. Back to Hedgewitch Cove. If she didn't, she had a sneaking suspicion history would repeat itself and she'd die all over again tonight.

No one in their right mind looked forward to that. While her previous death had been relatively painless, she knew that had been Luc's doing. That he'd intervened to save her that pain. Her gut said Luc wouldn't be there to help this time around.

His words about the contract her parents signed continued to play in her head. Those words were the only thing keeping her going. All she wanted to do was find a small out-of-the-way spot and sob.

That wasn't like her.

She wasn't a lick-her-wounds, cry-over-spilled-milk kind of girl. Yet that was what she'd been reduced to. That served to drive her, to make her want to push forward and figure a way out of her current predicament. She just needed to figure out what, exactly, had occurred.

She thought about the last thing she could recall. The antiques shop and Betty popped into her mind, as did the brooch and the coin. Both items were still tucked safely into the small pocket of her skirt. There was little room for doubt. They meant something. She just wasn't sure what.

She glanced over toward the street, following an urge she couldn't quite explain. As she did, she noticed the yellow cabs lining the road. That was nothing out of the ordinary for the city. Neither was all of the honking and shouting as people moved at a snail's pace in traffic.

One of the many cabs was breaking

from the pack and causing quite a stir as it attempted to blaze its own trail through the congestion. The passenger in the backseat turned his head to look at her and their gazes locked.

It couldn't be.

York?

How?

As she stared at the man with shoulder-length dark, wavy hair, his closely cut beard, and his dark eyes, her mouth formed an "O" and she shook her head in disbelief.

Whoever the man was, he looked identical to York.

For a second, the man appeared confused, and then his eyes widened. He threw his hands in the air and hit at the barrier between himself and the cab driver before he was suddenly out of the cab. He narrowly missed being hit by another taxi in the process but paid no mind to it all, his gaze locked firmly on her.

"Morgan?" he asked, his deep, Southern-tinged voice sounding like music to her ears.

She didn't know how it was he was in the

past with her. All she did know was that he represented her *real* home—Hedgewitch Cove.

She ran toward him, and he met her at the curb, grabbing her and lifting her off her feet in the process. Her feet dangled in the air as their bodies pressed firmly together. He spun her in a circle, holding her in a death grip, his body shaking slightly.

"Darlin', you scared years off me," he said, his mouth close to her ear.

The act of his warm breath skating over her skin sent a shiver of delight racing through her. Gasping, she squeezed him tighter, the tears breaking free in the process.

He set her on her feet but kept her close.

He cupped her face with his warm hands and stared down at her. Confusion knit his brow. "What happened? Did someone from the Collective hurt you? I'll kill them."

"What?" she asked, breathless.

He wiped the tears from her cheeks and then rubbed her exposed arms, clearly sensing she was cold. "Darlin', you're crying."

A choked laugh came from her. "I think

it's a result of a lot of emotions but at this very second, I'm crying because I'm happy you're here."

Relief shone on his handsome face. "You are? With what I said and what I accused you of, I wasn't sure you'd ever want to see me again."

"I was very hurt by what you said. I still am to a degree," she admitted, putting her hands to his steely chest as she did. "But blinking and finding myself trapped in the past kind of sucked the wind out of my offended sails."

He chuckled slightly. "You're freezing. Come on."

The cab he'd jumped out of was right where he'd left it, blocking traffic and earning a lot of honks and curses from fellow drivers. The door York had exited was still wide open. He led her back to it and helped guide her in.

The warmth of the vehicle hit her at once, helping to stop some of the bone-chilling cold she felt. She strongly suspected a large amount of it was shock and stress related. That, and it was clear to her that she wasn't as she had been in Hedgewitch Cove. She wasn't in spirit form.

No.

She was flesh and blood.

York eased into the cab next to her as best he could considering just how tall he was. The sight of the alpha male shark-shifter cramming himself into a city taxi for her sake only made her cry more.

He touched her chin lightly, directing her gaze to his. The next she knew, his lips were pressed to hers. Gasping, she gave him the opening he needed to take the kiss to another level, and he didn't disappoint. By the time he was done, she was a breathless puddle of hormones and tears.

His lips curved into a smile against hers. "I've wanted to do that for years. Pretty much since I was old enough to realize girls weren't icky."

"York?" she asked. He'd wanted to kiss her for years?

He put his finger to her lips, silencing her as he looked forward at the driver. "She'll tell you where to take us now."

Morgan's mind raced and the same urge

she'd had since arriving in the past was there. She needed to get to the contract, and if she knew her father at all, that was something he'd keep in the home safe, not at the office. "Home. He can take us to my parents' home."

"That the address on your identification?" asked York, pulling a billfold that looked suspiciously like the one she used to have from his back pocket.

Surprised, she touched it lightly, as if it might bite. "How did you get this?"

"Long story. The address the same?" he asked.

She nodded.

He inclined his head to the driver, who finally stopped blocking traffic and began to go.

Morgan grabbed York's T-shirt and fisted it as she looked him up and down. "How are you here? How did you find me? What's happening? Am I deader than normal?"

The cab driver glanced at the rearview mirror but didn't look shocked by her words. He probably heard a lot in his line of work.

York smoothed a strand of hair back from her face. "You are unbelievably gorgeous, darlin'."

A blush stole across her cheeks, heating her face.

He kissed the tip of her nose. "Best I didn't learn that until now though. I had a hard enough time focusing when I was only imagining what you looked like. Now that I know, I'm done for."

"York, be serious," she pleaded, her hands finding his.

"I *am*," he returned. "And to answer your question, Luc and Betty are behind the hows and whys. And you're the opposite of deader than normal. Not that dead was even your norm."

"What do you mean?" she questioned.

He leaned over, nuzzling his face to the crook of her neck. When he spoke, it was a soft whisper against her ear. "You're a real girl, Pinocchio."

She was about to question him more but thought harder on how she'd felt since finding herself in the past. A small yelp came from her as she understood what he was saying. "I'm alive?"

The comment came out louder than she'd meant and earned her a raised brow from the cab driver as he glanced in the rearview mirror once more.

Snickering, York kept his mouth where it was. "You are, darlin'. Want to have your mind *really* blown?"

"There's more?" she asked, unsure she could handle anything else. Already she'd gone back in time and somehow managed to come back to life. Anything else might just do her in.

He kissed her earlobe and laughed softly again. "You're my mate."

A nervous giggle escaped her a second before she considered his words more. As she did, her fingers went to the coin in her pocket. She withdrew it and held it out for York to see.

He eased it from her hand and studied it. His thumb scraped over the magic symbols before he turned it and grinned at the sight of the state of New York and the Statue of Liberty. He then looked upward.

"Remind me to thank Mémé when we get home."

"York!" she shouted, causing the driver to jolt somewhat. "Sorry."

York was grinning like the cat that ate the canary. Or, in his case, the shark that munched on the surfer. He looked downright giddy that he'd been cursed by his grandmother.

She stared at him in disbelief. "We're…?"

"We are," he said with a wink. "This is perfect. See, *I'm your man* and *you're always on my mind*. Plus, you have me *wrapped around your finger*."

When she realized he was stringing together song titles from the '80s, something he'd taken to doing several months back, she found herself smiling. The man got her on a level no other person ever really had.

He put his forehead to hers. "Now, what do you say we find some contract Luc mentioned and find a way back home?"

She nodded, tearing up more, overcome with a swell of happiness. "Yes. That."

He slinked his arm around her and held

her close as they drove through the city. She caught him giving the side-eye to more than one person walking down the street. No surprise since the era was full of a lot of colorful clothing and people.

There was a man in short shorts, on roller skates, no shirt, holding a boombox over one shoulder as he did circles on the sidewalk. His hair was permed, and he wore a yellow headband. His mustache was rather epic in a very Tom Selleck-worthy kind of way.

York's eyes widened. "I'm not gonna be expected to dress like that to fit in here, am I?"

"No," she said quickly, doing her best to keep from laughing outright at the look of horror on his face. "But I think a nice pair of jam pants and a muscle shirt would be hot on you."

He jerked around to stare at her. "Really?"

She tipped to one side, laughter erupting from her like lava from a volcano. The expression on his face was priceless. "I should say yes. With all the teasing you've done to me over the years, it would serve you right."

"Sweet Lord above, for a second I thought you were serious, and I'd be stuck runnin' around town with my britches up my hind end, wheeling about, looking like a chicken with its head cut off. If it's all right by you, I think I'll just stick to jeans and boots."

She could take the cowboy out of the South, but she couldn't take the South out of the cowboy. That much was clear.

Her hand found his powerful thigh, and she put her head against his shoulder, enjoying being held by him. For as much time as she'd spent avoiding showing herself to him over the years, all she wanted to do was stay where he could see her and be close to him.

Chapter Ten

YORK PAID the driver and stepped away from the taxi to stand near his punk-rock girl. She was as opposite as one could get from him, yet she was absolutely perfect. He felt right and whole being near her knowing the truth—that she was his mate.

He just hoped she'd be okay with being claimed by him.

They'd yet to discuss the matter in-depth and he wasn't sure what her response would be. First, he needed to find the contract Luc said to grab and then find a way to get his woman back to the future they'd come from.

"McFly moment," he said, as he glanced up at the large brownstone home before him.

He was no expert on New York City real estate, but he knew the place cost a pretty penny. "If you're loaded and you know it, clap your hands." He wanted to ease some of the fear he sensed coming off Morgan.

She lifted a brow and stared at his hands. "Well? You planning to clap? Your family pretty much owns a town."

She had a point. He clapped, and she smiled, reaching out and taking his hand in hers. She gave a gentle squeeze and took a deep breath. "We're doing this then? We're going in?"

"We are," he replied.

"What if my parents are in there? They're supposed to be in the south of France, but I don't know anything anymore. What if they aren't?"

A calculated smile touched his lips as he thought about all the things he'd do to her parents. They all involved pain and torture and then some more pain.

"From the expression on your face, I'm going to say you're really hoping they are in there," she said with a small snort. "Do me a favor, break expensive things. It will upset my mother more than anything else you could ever think to do. Or growl at her demon-dog."

"She has a pet demon?" asked York, thinking more about it.

"No, but it's as mean as can be."

He knew she was stalling. "You know, I never asked what kind of supernatural you are...erm...were, no wait, *are*."

She grumbled. "That made my head hurt, yet I followed it somehow. And to answer your question, I'm not one."

"What do you mean, you're not one?" Of course, she was supernatural. She was his mate.

"Does being a kind-of ghost count?" she asked, and he realized she didn't know the truth of it all.

He lifted their joined hands and kissed her knuckles one by one. "Darlin', do you understand that no one is a member of the Collective who isn't supernatural to some degree? And that would mean your parents are. If they are, that means you are."

She stepped closer to him and squeezed his hand tight. "Ohmygod, what am I?"

He laughed. "My mate. And before you think too hard on that statement, you should know that in order to be my mate, you've got to be more than human."

Morgan tried to wiggle her hand free from him, and he caught the impression if he dared let go, she'd bolt like a jackrabbit. He bent and kissed the tip of her nose once more. He really wanted to simply stare at her for hours upon hours, memorizing every line and curve of her face and body, seeing as how today was the first day he'd ever been allowed to see her, but he knew they had work to do.

"We need to get that contract Luc mentioned," confessed York—a second before he got the distinct feeling they were being watched.

Playing it cool, he turned his head slightly to glance around for anyone who looked suspicious. The street Morgan lived on wasn't as crowded as the ones they'd been on before, but that didn't mean they were alone. While the number of people passing by more than likely seemed relatively small in comparison to the rest of New York City, it was a whole lot of folks when pitted against Hedgewitch Cove.

Then there was the glaringly obvious fact that everyone looked at least slightly suspect to York. How could they not with their choice of hairstyles? What were people in the '80s thinking? And how did they get so many on board with horrible perms and so much hairspray? He didn't even want to get into the clothing they wore. Did they own mirrors?

"You didn't hear a word I said, did you?" asked Morgan.

York cleared his throat and looked down at her. "Um, yes?"

She groaned. "Luc mentioned a contract to me the night I died. Okay, which is tonight, but you get what I mean."

He nodded. She wouldn't die if he could help it.

His magic stirred deep in him, making itself known. With it came the deep-set knowledge that if he dared to stop what was to happen, there would be a worse hell to endure.

He had to let the Morgan of the past die. Had to let events play out as they were meant to. Luc's reminder that there were two versions of Morgan here was the only thing that helped York even entertain the possibility of permitting events to unfold as they once had. He didn't understand the inner workings of time travel and having it explained in detail wouldn't have helped him any.

Not when it came to his mate.

The woman he loved.

Allowing any version of her to be killed went against every ounce of his being. The alpha in him wanted to lash out at everything and everyone who dared to think of harming his mate, and the man in him wanted to hold Morgan and never let go.

"He said my parents signed some contract with the Collective that concerned me," she told him, drawing him from his thoughts. "He made sure I knew that if I was ever given the chance to get the contract, I should take it."

"Then let's find us that contract, darlin'."

She went up the front steps and bent, lifting a small flowerpot to expose a spare key. The key placement didn't seem like the best security measure, especially living in the city, but what did he know? He never locked his doors back home. He didn't have to. Anyone dumb enough to try breaking in would find themselves looking at a partially shifted shark.

Pretty decent crime deterrent.

Within seconds, Morgan was entering the home, and York kept his body behind hers to block her from who or whatever he was sure was watching them. He wasn't sure if they were friend or foe, but he did know they were close. For now, he'd permit them to linger but if they made a move to harm his woman, he'd rip them to shreds and not lose a wink of sleep over it.

Morgan meant that much to him.

Mine.

The word bounced around in his head before settling in his chest, warming the area. He felt like a lovesick teenager, not a grown man. In many ways, he'd always been something of a lovestruck fool when it came to Morgan. How had he not seen who she was to him years ago?

"Coming?" asked Morgan, holding the door open for him.

He entered and was instantly hit with the faint scents of other animals. If he was right, he could smell the hedgehog and bat Luc had mentioned, and something that could be the dog Morgan mentioned her mother having. Though the smell was off to the point he couldn't pinpoint what it was. Maybe Morgan's mother put perfume on her dog.

As he stared around the ornate furnishings in the home, he had a hunch he was right about the perfume. As they went through the house, York couldn't help but take note of the lack of family photos. There was a portrait of a man and a woman above the fireplace. The people depicted matched the picture he'd seen of her parents.

There was no sign that they even had a daughter.

How had Morgan ended up with such a

big heart coming from such a sterile environment?

Sure, his family wasn't hurting for cash, but they weren't anything like these people. They were warm and loving. They employed a large number of the people in the town, paid fair wages, and were always giving back to the community. They weren't fancy folks, but they were good people.

The deeper Morgan took him into the home, the more he wanted to hunt down her parents and spend a week locked away in a room with them. When he was done, they'd know just how much their daughter meant to him and how much they should have cherished her when they'd had the chance. They were Collective members, so they more than likely wouldn't ever see the error of their ways.

There was a clanging from what York suspected was the kitchen area.

Morgan ran in that direction.

The woman had no sense. He was trying to keep her safe while she was busy running toward loud noises.

York caught her around the waist a

second before she'd have made it all the way into the large all-white kitchen.

A short, plump woman stood before the stove stirring something in a pot. The older woman's hair was pulled up in a tight bun, showing a mix of gray, white, and black hair. She was wearing a red sweater with a pair of black slacks and matching orthopedic shoes with tiny blue hearts on the sides. The apron she worse also had the tiniest of heart patterns.

She glanced over at York and Morgan, grinning as she did.

"Millie!" exclaimed Morgan.

"Sweetheart, I thought you were headed out to eat and see that show you've been talking about nonstop for days."

This was the famed Mildred? Like Betty, she didn't look like much of a threat. But like Betty, York was guessing the woman could be downright deadly. It struck him then that Morgan didn't yet know of Millie's connection to Betty.

His mate ran at Millie, tossing her arms around the woman, closing her eyes as she did. "I missed you."

Millie, who was just shy of five feet tall, wrapped her arms around Morgan's waist. "Well, sweetheart, you just saw me at breakfast. Are you okay?"

Morgan nodded and teared up once more.

York knew it was emotional for her to see someone she clearly cared about after so long. He wanted to give them time alone, but the clock was ticking. He didn't know how long he had to get the contract and put things back on track, but York strongly suspected he was already pushing that time limit.

Morgan drew back ever so slightly from Millie, her attention going to the brooch Millie was wearing on her red sweater.

York had seen one that looked identical on Betty before.

"W-where did you get that?" asked Morgan.

Millie touched it lightly. "Oh, this? I've had it for years and years."

"Did Luc give that to you?" questioned Morgan.

"He did. He's such a sweet boy," said Millie.

York knew Morgan would put it all together soon enough, and he intended to fill in all the details he could, with the limited amount of information he had, but they needed to find the contract.

He bent slightly. "Darlin', we need to handle that thing. Remember?"

Millie eyed him cautiously. "And who might you be?"

He extended his hand to her. "New York Peugeot, ma'am."

She lifted her chin slightly and narrowed her gaze on him. "Are you now?"

"I am," he returned.

"Millie, what's for dinner tonight? Barton and his business associates will be dining with us," said a shrill voice from down the hall.

Morgan gasped. "Mom and Dad are home? I thought they were in France still."

Millie shrugged. "They got home just after you left this morning. Your father is in his study with more of his friends. Best you and your friend there head on upstairs and stay clear of your father and his business."

It was easy to hear the note of concern in Millie's voice. She wanted Morgan safe.

"Millie? Can you hear me," asked a woman who didn't look much older than Morgan as she came around the corner into the kitchen. Her hair was piled high on her head, and long diamond earrings hung from each ear. She was in a puffy-collared pink silk shirt and a pair of gray slacks. She had on four-inch pink heels. She drew up short when she saw Morgan and York there. "Morgan? What are you doing home?"

York's temper began to poke through, and he made a move to go at the woman, only to find Morgan planting herself in his path.

"I forgot the tickets to the show tonight. My date and I needed to grab them. We won't be long. Glad to see that you're home," said Morgan, sounding as if she were choking on the words. She took York's hand in hers and held it in a death grip.

He understood Morgan needed

emotional support and to show a united front. He had no issues with that. He'd shout his loyalty to her from the rooftops if required.

Morgan's mother stared at York, saying nothing for the longest time. There was a glint in her eyes that only a fellow predator could appreciate and fully comprehend. As a shark-shifter, York was certainly a predator. Something deep down told him Muffy was one as well.

A small poodle sauntered into the kitchen, focused on him, and bared its teeth before going straight to Morgan's mother.

The woman bent and lifted the dog in her arms. She stroked its head as she looked at York once more. "You don't seem like my daughter's type."

Morgan's shoulders went back. "He's exactly my type, Muffy. In fact, he's perfect for me. It's like it's fate or something."

Muffy didn't appear fazed by her daughter's outburst. She just continued to pet the dog. "Do you have a name, Mr. Perfect?"

Millie grinned. "New York Peugeot."

"Peugeot?" questioned Muffy. "As in Walden? Any relation? Cousin perhaps?"

York's jaw set. "Yes. As in Walden. And, um, *yes*, I'm related. You can call me York, ma'am."

"I see," said Muffy.

Millie looked downright ecstatic. "Good news, yes?"

"Something is different. What is it?" asked Muffy.

"I'm trying a new recipe," said Millie, her eyes sparkling. "It's an *old* family favorite."

York nearly coughed. If Millie was anything like Betty, that meant there were body parts in the food.

The dog continued to growl at York.

He could see what Morgan meant. It did seem nothing but mean. He let his shark up enough to alert other animals in the area that he was the top predator. The dog began to whimper and then yelp before hiding in Muffy's arms.

She glanced down at the dog and then toward York. The edges of her mouth drew upward as she tipped her head. "She senses you're dominant. The alpha male. I can see what my daughter likes about you."

Chapter Eleven

DID he just hear Morgan's mother correctly? Had she referred to him as dominant and an alpha male? Did that mean she knew the truth about him? That he was a shark-shifter? Or did she sense his magic side? What if she caught on that he was a hunter as well? Would she try something foolish? If she did, would Morgan understand what he'd have to do to the woman?

Sure, she was evil and had apparently given her daughter over to the Collective, but that didn't mean she wasn't, in the end, Morgan's mother. The woman who had given birth to his mate. If York was forced to do the unthinkable, could Morgan ever forgive him? Could he forgive himself?

"Mother?" asked Morgan, sounding surprised by the woman's words. "What do you mean by dominant?"

Muffy bent and set the dog down on the floor. She touched its back. "Be a good little demon and let me know if any of them leave the study."

York eased Morgan back slightly. He turned his head somewhat but didn't dare take his gaze from Muffy or Millie as he spoke to Morgan. "I think you were right about your mother's poodle being a demon. I thought something smelled off with it."

Millie grinned. "It's a hellhound. Small, but mighty."

"Like you," said Muffy to Millie, making it clear they were friends. "Like you. You're small but mighty. But you're not a hellhound."

"Shut the front door," said Morgan, her voice barely there as she skimmed her fingers over York's hand, heating his skin. "It *is* evil! I knew it! It's vicious."

"No, sweetie," countered Millie. There

was a gentleness to her voice that said she was practiced at calming Morgan.

Part of York wanted to take notes for use later. It would more than likely come in handy with as much as he managed to get under his mate's skin.

"It's just following your mother's orders," said Millie.

"Yes, so like I said, evil," returned Morgan.

Millie glanced at Muffy, giving the woman a knowing look. "She'll understand in the end. It will all work out. You'll see."

With that, the dog hurried off in the other direction, walking as if it didn't have a care in the world. York had seen Luc's hellhound, Furfur, in action, and it was always a sight to behold. It also had a thing for stealing body parts from the cemetery only to rebury them later. Somehow, York couldn't picture the poodle doing anything close to that. A leg bone would be bigger than the thing.

"What's going on?" demanded York.

"I like your friend," said Muffy' to Morgan. "Has he claimed you yet?"

Morgan swallowed loudly. "Y-you know what he is?"

Her mother inclined her head. "A shifter of some sort. I can't tell what kind. He doesn't smell like a cat or a wolf to me. Something unique?"

York shrugged. "You can say that, yes. But it would depend on your definition of unique. I've seen how you decorate. We might not have the same definitions."

Morgan shook her head slightly. "York, now isn't the time for jokes."

"Good a time as any," he countered, wanting to kiss her but holding back.

It was difficult.

"Mother, how do you know he's a shifter, and what do you mean by his smell?" asked Morgan. "He doesn't smell like anything to me."

"Is that so?" asked Muffy. "Nothing at all? Really?"

York was interested in Morgan's response, so he stared down at her.

She shrugged. "Well, I guess he smells like the ocean to me. Like saltwater and a light breeze. Fresh. Good. Very good."

"You smell downright delicious to me," added York quickly, earning him a lot of raised brows in the roomful of women.

He reddened.

Muffy laughed. "You're attracted to her. That's good. Am I to assume you're some sort of marine-life shifter?"

He took a moment before answering, sizing her up as he did. "I am."

Millie bit her lower lip, looking hungry. "Shark."

He'd seen Betty eat part of a squid-shifter before. He didn't want to know if Millie found shark appetizing.

Muffy laughed. "Of course. Sharks are powerful and fierce. Traits that are needed to stand against the enemy and prevail. Tell me, are you a good man, York?"

"He's a great man," said Morgan on his behalf. "Cocky and too sure of himself, but other than that, he's amazing."

"Uh, thanks, darlin'."

She blinked up at him and looked too adorable to resist. The next he knew, he bent and stole a chaste kiss from her lips. He cleared his throat and stood tall once more.

Morgan touched her lips gingerly, her green gaze set on him.

Didn't the woman understand the picture she painted? How much he wanted to toss her over his shoulder and carry her off into the sunset?

When she bit at her lower lip, he knew then that she had no clue just how much power she had over him.

Muffy nodded to Millie in a way that left little room for misinterpretation. They were co-conspirators in something. "I think it's time."

"I think you're right," said Millie, putting her fingers to her lips and whistling sharply.

He'd assumed Millie would be on their side, not alerting the enemy to their presence.

York grabbed Morgan and thrust her behind his body, going on high alert. If Collective members were in the home and wanted Morgan, they'd need to get through him first, and few people could claim that victory.

Millie snorted at his actions. "Sweetie, you can relax. There is no need to flex your dominant muscles. We know you'd do anything to protect her."

Muffy clasped her hands together and brought them to her lips, tearing up in the process. "As it should be, with you being her mate and all. Just the type of man I'd want for my daughter to spend eternity with. This is perfect."

"Pardon me?" he asked, sure his ears were playing tricks on him.

Muffy grinned. "You look ready to challenge the world. That's an admirable quality in a mate."

York glanced at Morgan. "I thought she was evil."

"Me too," said Morgan, shaking her head. "I'm really lost right now."

Muffy extended an arm a second before a huge black bat came flying into the kitchen. It was what some termed a vampire bat. It hooked onto Muffy's forearm and hung upside down, staring over at Morgan with large, curious eyes. It didn't smell like any bat he'd been around before. But it did smell a lot like a vampire now that it was closer to him.

"Booker!" shouted Morgan, making a move to go for the bat.

York caught her arm. "No. That's no ordinary pet."

She offered an annoyed look. "I know. It's a bat. Not too many people have them for pets. Luc gave him to me."

Millie grinned at Muffy before her gaze found Morgan. "Actually, your mother is who put Booker in Luc's path years ago. She needed to have someone she trusted fully around you at all times without alerting her family, or your father and *his* family. She went to her vampire den and asked that an old debt be repaid. Booker has done as she asked for years now, Morgan. So has Spike, your hedgehog. He owed me a favor, so he agreed to get cursed into animal form for a time."

"Wait, what?" asked Morgan, somehow managing to pale more. "Booker is a vampire, and Spike is a, um, what is Spike?"

"Part shifter, part human, and part demon," said Millie and Muffy in unison as if they'd rehearsed it many times before.

Morgan rubbed her head. "This is too

much to absorb. Muffy, you barely acknowledge me and signed a contract to give my soul to the Collective. Why would you care if I have protectors or not? Making sure the sacrifice is whole and ready for transfer? That is what that contract you signed called me, right? A sacrifice?"

York growled.

Millie shook her head. "Calm down, New York. I'm likely to take offense. *You* wouldn't want that."

"Betty made it sound like you were on our side," said York. "Not with the Collective."

Morgan faced him. "Betty knows Millie?"

"Millie is Mildred," offered York.

Morgan's mouth dropped open. "She's Betty's sister?"

He nodded.

She swayed. "I ate her cooking all growing up! Did I eat zombie parts?"

Muffy laughed. "No. Only Millie eats those. I don't eat food. I drink blood in my wineglasses and push food around on my plate. Since you weren't born with an aversion to the sun and a need for blood, like me, and showed no signs of being a dark wizard like your father, I pushed to raise you as human. I had hoped it would keep the Collective from wanting you. You and your soul are only important to them if you're powerful. If you're like us. All along they've sworn you are."

Muffy was a vampire, and Morgan's father was a dark wizard?

Morgan slammed into York. He twisted around, catching and steadying her as she took in the news, her mother was a creature of the night, and her father was a mage. That meant Morgan had vampire and magic in her as well on some level.

"My mind is officially blown," said Morgan. "For thirty years I've thought my mother was evil, and while I'm not sure whose side she's on, I now know she's a vampire. And it looks like my dad is apparently a dark wizard. I don't even know what that is. Doesn't sound good. All aboard the crazy train."

Muffy stepped closer to Morgan, but York stiffened.

Millie nodded at him. "She won't hurt her. She loves her with all her being and has gone out of her way to try to stop the actions of Morgan's father. He's not a good person."

"Neither is she, according to Luc," said Morgan, pointing at her mother.

Muffy sighed. "Morgan, for the Collective to fully believe I'm all in on what they forced me to sign, I had to let everyone think I'm a believer too. That I'm part of that cult of insanity and evil. I'm not. I was born into it and wanted to keep it far from you. I'm not the only member of my vampire den to see the error of the old ways. Booker saw too. I'm sorry I wasn't able to do a better job, and I'm sorry you've had to suffer for my shortcomings. I'm assuming you're from the future. Thirty years?"

"How did you know that?" demanded York. It was too good of a guess to be random. Information was power, and he needed to know everything Muffy and Millie did.

Millie smiled wide. "A hunter friend of mine from Maine gave me a crystal ball that predicts important events in the future. This ball is set to work for people I care about like family. I've known Muffy for centuries. She's like a daughter to me. Morgan is like a granddaughter. The crystal ball showed Muffy and me all the signs. Showed us what would happen if we dared to interfere with what is set to happen to the Morgan of this time. Bad things. Really bad things. The best we could do was get word to Luc through the grapevine that you were in danger. He's always loved you like your father should have. He'll do right. He'll step in and protect you until you can be united with your mate."

York took a deep breath. "He *does* step in and protect her."

"Good," said Muffy her eyes moist. "Very good. I hated betraying him. I hated lying to him and making him think I was against my own daughter."

Morgan made a small noise that indicated she was having trouble processing everything.

York couldn't blame her. Time travel was giving him a migraine.

Muffy nodded as if she understood as

well. "It's all confusing. I know. Tampering with time always is. Dealing with two versions of one's self. Knowing that if you undo one thread, it could unravel the whole ball of time. It's why very few demons can do it. Millie and her sisters have the ability to some extent, but it's not endless, and they can only do it a few times in their extremely long lives."

Morgan stepped back fast, and York feared she'd faint. "This has been a peculiar day, and I live with the devil, some demons, and a bunch of spirits, so that should tell you something."

Muffy beamed. "Oh, Luc does, erm, *did* take you in and watch over you then? I'm sorry. I'm not sure how to refer to things."

"Any way you want is fine," said Morgan softly. "And yes, Luc has been with never ever since I died. I live with him full-time down in Louisiana. At his inn there."

It was easy to see Muffy was fighting her emotions. "It looks like he took very good care of your body. It's not aged a day and doesn't show any signs of injury. I swear if he weren't already destined for a natural-born hunter, I'd have tried to charm that man myself. He's a catch."

Luc's mate was a hunter? That was news to York. He didn't think the devil had a mate.

"Luc says if she's hurt here and now, he can't help her. That she'll be gone for good," said York fast, the need to get everyone on the same page great. "He told us to find a contract."

Muffy nodded. "Yes. I know the one he's talking about. It's in my husband's study. In the vault there. I can get to it, but I'll need a distraction. My husband is currently entertaining high-ranking Collective members. They're celebrating something, and since Morgan from the past dies tonight, I'm going to assume the party is because they think they're getting her soul tonight. Let's be sure that doesn't happen. If they get her soul, the Morgan standing here with us now, can't ever come to be."

Millie lifted a hand, and one finger extended as a long, dagger-like nail appeared from the end of it. "What did you have in mind?"

Gasping, Morgan grabbed for York. "I did *not* see that coming."

York wrapped his arm tighter around his mate and kissed the top of her head. "Figured you'd be used to the strange and unusual by now. All that time spent around me."

She patted his chest. "This is a lot to take in."

Chapter Twelve

YORK COULD MORE than understand why Morgan was having a hard time with it all. She was right. It was a lot to take in.

Muffy rubbed the belly of the bat and bent, whispering something in its ear. There was a poof of black smoke, and then a tall, built man appeared wearing a tailored, dark gray suit, complete with a vest, pocket watch, and matching top hat. Long black hair hung just past the man's shoulders.

He looked at Morgan and winked.

She swayed, and York held firmer to her, keeping her upright. "My bat is a hot guy."

Muffy smiled. "I'm sure Booker is pleased to hear you think he's attractive.

He's always been something of a ladies' man."

York stiffened. "That guy had unlimited access to my mate?"

Booker tipped his head and removed his hat. When he smiled, he flashed fang. "I did. Seeing as how she is my great-great-great-great-niece, I think it's safe to say there was nothing inappropriate afoot."

"Does he look over thirty-five to you?" asked Morgan of York. "I'm having a hard time wrapping my head around the knowledge that my pet bat is really an immortal vampire."

York rolled his eyes. "I don't like him."

"You don't know him," argued Morgan.

"Neither do you. Five minutes ago, you thought Booker was your pet," snapped York. "Look at him. Seems awfully haughty if you ask me."

Morgan squared her shoulders and put her hands on her hips. "I'll have you know that I trust him. He was a great, erm, pet."

Booker flashed a wide smile. One that York knew the ladies would fall for. He, himself, was great with the opposite sex. He knew what they went for. And Booker fit the bill.

He opened his mouth to give Morgan a piece of his mind but stopped when he noticed the way she was glaring at him. There was a fierceness there, just below the surface, almost daring him to push further. In that second, his shark side did its version of tucking its tail between its legs and retreating. It didn't like having its mate angry with him.

Neither did York. "Um, shutting up now."

Morgan seemed pleased as punch at his response. "Good boy."

"And he called *me* a pet," said Booker with a huff.

York growled, ready and willing to take on the man. There was something about him that rubbed York the wrong way.

"Making friends again?" asked a man with long red hair that was pulled back at the nape of his neck and a thick matching red beard as he entered the kitchen. He had on a pair of dress pants but nothing else, leaving him barefoot and shirtless. His honed form and how he carried himself alerted York that the man was more than likely a shifter.

The newcomer touched the pants he was in, his attention on Muffy. "Took these from your husband's wardrobe. Thought it best I not walk down naked."

Muffy nodded. "Thank you, Spike. But you should know, it is not a hardship seeing you without clothing."

That was Spike?

York felt faint.

He could only hope the redhead was also related to Morgan. He did not want to compete for his mate's affection with that man.

"*Holy wow*, my hedgehog is a hottie too," said Morgan with a breathless sigh.

"Tell me he's her uncle, please," said York to Muffy.

Millie giggled. "Spike? No. He's a demon. No relation of mine either, but our clans are on good terms. He owed me a favor or two, and when he learned Morgan was in danger, he wanted to help any way he could."

Spike stretched his arms above his head, showing off his form and his height.

They were identical to York's.

Morgan and Muffy stared at the act as if they wanted it to be recorded for playback at a later date.

Tugging lightly on his mate's arm, York cleared his throat. "Morgan, try not to stare."

"I can't look away," said Morgan.

Muffy nodded. "Difficult. I know."

Millie's lip curled. "If you think the fact that his base human form is attractive, then sure. But I much rather prefer my men with two or three heads and horns."

Morgan stared harder at Spike. "He slept in bed with me for years. I never knew my sweet hedgehog was really so impressive."

"He's not *that* impressive," interjected York in a voice that more than announced his jealousy.

Millie touched the counter lightly. "You're close to challenging the men in the room when your focus should be on the enemy in the house. These men aren't it."

"From where I'm standing, Spike is a front-runner," said York before thinking better of it.

"What is your deal?" demanded Morgan.

"He's got a taste of the green-eyed monster. Otherwise known as being jealous," said Muffy, seeming amused. "What man would be fine knowing his significant other won the heart of a man who looks like Spike?"

"It's because I rubbed Spike's belly in hedgehog form, isn't it?" asked Morgan in a silly manner that eased some of the tension in the room. "Is Spike your real name?"

"No," replied the demon-shifter. "But it's long, boring, and very Latin. So, Spike is what I've gone by for hundreds of years."

Morgan pointed between Booker and Spike. "One of you appeared fully dressed. Can you both do that when you change?"

Booker licked his lower lip. "Just me. Spike gets dressed the old-fashioned way. He shows up in his birthday suit."

"Cool," returned Morgan.

York groaned more. "I need a Collective

member to break. Fast. Before my shark side decides to come out and play."

Millie smiled wide. "Goodie. We have extras on hand. But first, let us distract them all, and Muffy can grab the contract. It's best Morgan be kept safely out of the way."

"I agree. But I'll handle the Collective members," said York. "They want to harm my mate. That means they've got a can of whoop—"

Morgan raised a hand, cutting him off. "We get the point."

Booker snorted. "Let him go on. It always amuses me how much shifter males feel the need to announce just how alpha they are. Negates the point they're making."

York and Spike growled.

It only served to make Booker laugh more.

Millie nodded to York. "Morgan needs to be protected at all costs. Some of the Collective members could easily steal her soul without much thought or effort. Her father will sacrifice her in the blink of an eye. He won't risk his standing in the organization or his power."

"What does this contract do, and why is it so important?" asked York.

Muffy took a deep breath and lowered her gaze. Shame was evident on her face.

Booker rubbed her back lightly. "You cannot blame yourself. He tricked you. He tricked all of us."

"I should have seen through the lies," she confessed. "I was blinded by what I thought was love. And I wanted to be normal. To know what it feels like to stand in the noonday sun. When he pushed me to sign it, the idea of ever having a child with him seemed absurd. He's not my mate. I didn't think it would ever happen, so I didn't know there was a real risk. I wouldn't have let him push me to sign it had I known Morgan would come to be."

Millie sighed. "Barton used his magic and borrowed from even darker powers to make sure the two of you had a child together. He needed a tribute to offer to the Collective. He was too worried about money and power."

"So was I," confessed Muffy. "I wish I could do it over again."

"If you did, Morgan would never come to be," said Millie in a way that said she was sure of her words. "It killed you to have to keep her at arm's length all of her life. I know you wanted to hold her, to love her, to let her know she is loved."

Morgan gasped. "Muffy wanted to hold me? Are you *sure*?"

Booker nodded. "She's sure. Your mother loves you, Morgan. When she learned the lengths that your father would go to get what he wanted, she found ways to alert Luc. She couldn't go to him outright, or the Collective would have known. She had to find creative ways around them."

Morgan stilled. "She made Luc my godfather, didn't she?"

"Yes," said Booker. "She'd been friends with him for centuries before your father came into the picture. Luc tried to steer her clear of Barton."

"I was a fool," said Muffy. "Passion clouded my mind. And in truth, I wasn't the best person back then. Luc was always disappointed in my actions. He gave up on me after Morgan was born. I still don't know why he agreed to be her godfather."

"Because he sensed something in her," said Millie. "A connection she'd have to a family who has a destiny woven with his."

Was she talking about York's family? He nearly asked but held his tongue.

Muffy wiped her eyes and took a deep breath. "Enough tears and regret. The important thing now is getting the contract that says Morgan willingly offers her soul to the Collective as a sacrifice."

"It says I what?" asked Morgan.

"You didn't sign it," said Muffy. "Your father did for you. He signed your name with his power. It's a spell that can be broken so long as you're alive."

Morgan put her hand up. "I'm dead. The Collective killed me on this night thirty years ago. After the concert the me of my past and your present is attending."

Booker and Spike both went on high alert.

York found himself disliking them a little less, knowing how much they wanted to keep his mate safe.

Muffy's eyes moistened before she began to cry outright. "The you of now? She dies tonight?"

"Yes," said York, his hand finding his mate's shoulder in a show of support.

Millie looked pained. "Muffy, it has to be. If we find a way to change that, Morgan might never meet York. The ripple effects could be devastating. We have to let her die tonight so that she can return to us just like she is now."

Morgan ran her hands through her hair, stress evident. "You're saying Dad magically forged my name?"

Muffy nodded.

"No one caught on? I mean, I was like brand new to the world when he did it. My writing ability really didn't come about for another six years or so." Morgan touched her stomach next, and worry radiated from her. "It can't be like legally binding or anything, right?"

Booker, Spike, and York shared looks that said they more than understood how underhanded the Collective could be. No human court of law could touch them, and they knew it.

York drew Morgan to him. He gave her a gentle squeeze. "We'll get the contract, and we'll handle it."

"How? Apparently, my father is some dark wizard." She put her palms to his chest. "That's bad, right?"

"It's not great, darlin'," answered York. "Could be worse."

She didn't look as if she believed him. "How so?"

"I'm thinking."

That earned him a nervous laugh and a quick hug from Morgan.

"But they said I had to be alive to get out of the contract," said Morgan, sounding so young that it was easy to forget that she'd had thirty years dead under her belt.

He smoothed her hair back from her eyes. "Darlin', you're alive now. That's what matters. You're flesh. You're blood."

"And you can be killed," said Booker sternly. "That means you need to stay far from your father and his men right now."

"Agreed," said Muffy. "York, take my

daughter up to her room. It's warded from evil. That is why I can't enter it. Neither can her father or his men."

"You warded my room against your-self?" asked Morgan.

Millie let out a long, slow breath. "No, child. She warded it to protect you, and that left her being blocked from entering. See, while she loves you, she did, in the end, sign something that can cause you great harm. She knew the risk of warding your room. If she'd have gotten her way, the whole house would be warded for you."

"True," said Spike. "Muffy has always wanted the best for you. Your father is another story."

Millie nodded. "Now, either your mate can take you up to your room, or Booker and Spike can." She stared at York. "Killing things, or alone time with your mate? You decide."

York grabbed his woman's hand. "Where is your room?"

Muffy pointed in the direction of a set of stairs, and York practically dragged Morgan with him. He hadn't meant to. He was just that excited to both get a second alone with her and keep her safe.

She hurried along behind him as he raced up the stairs.

"Last door on the right," she said.

He went right for it, and when he opened the door, he was struck with a room that felt exactly like the Morgan he knew. It was done in all white with a huge red stop sign affixed to the wall. Posters from bands were hung as well as a movie poster from the film *JAWS*.

He chuckled. "Got a thing for sharks?"

She eased into the room and then shut and locked the door.

He took stock of her shirt and what it said. "Oh, sharks and *New York*. Nice. Good to be loved."

He'd meant it as a joke, but the way she looked at him was off.

"Morgan?"

"You! It was you at the concert all those years ago. You're the cowboy who came up to me and chased off this creepy guy."

He had no idea what she was talking about. "Darlin'?"

"You end up at the concert tonight, York. Thirty years ago, you came to me there," she insisted, standing firm. Her eyes widened. "You told me you wished that you could change it all for me, and that it would all end okay. Then you said you loved me."

York nearly denied having anything remotely close to love for her, but he stopped. He did love her. A lot. And there was no better time than the present to tell her as much. He took her hands in his and lowered his head. "Morgan, are you okay with that? With me loving you?"

Her lips pursed, and he knew she was thinking about what he'd asked. That didn't stop him from doing what felt right. He kissed her, half expecting her to realize he wasn't good enough for her and to push him away.

When she bit at his lower lip and went for his shirt, York couldn't hide his elation. But now wasn't the time for it all.

He caught her wrists. "Morgan, I want you, darlin'. More than anything in the world, but we need to get the contract and you out of here. I want you safe."

Nodding, she kept tugging at his shirt and went to her tiptoes. "And everything in me is shouting about how you need to make this official to make sure that happens."

"The second we're back to our time, I'm gonna make you mine," he promised. He kissed her temple. "Stay here. I'm going to help the others. Don't leave this room."

York's hand found the bedroom door handle, and his power flared. It sent a jolt through him, carrying with it the knowledge that if he didn't claim her now, she wouldn't be returning with him when the time came. That she'd be forever lost to him.

That was unacceptable.

He glanced at her bed, which had black bedding. His little punk rocker was a firecracker. And she was his. The time had come to make sure of that.

He bent and scooped her off her feet, rushing her toward the bed.

"York?" she squeaked. "I thought you said we were waiting until we're back home."

"Changed my mind," he said with a waggle of his brows.

Chapter Thirteen

MORGAN WATCHED as York paced the room. She was still in a state of shock over what had happened between them. It had been wonderful. York had surprised her with how sweet and tender he could be.

Her time in Hedgewitch Cove had taught her a number of things about supernaturals. Namely, how mating did and did not work. And she was most certainly mated to York now.

Husband and wife.

That would take some getting used to, but she knew they'd figure it all out. After all, they loved one another and had for some time. Didn't hurt that Fate had their back, making them mates and all.

The day had been nothing short of a whirlwind, but she wouldn't change anything. Okay, she'd maybe not have the Collective after her again, but other than that, no. She'd gotten to see Millie again, learn that her pets were more than fine, and find out that her mother wasn't evil after all.

Just seriously misguided.

"Please sit down, you're giving me a headache," said Morgan, touching her stomach gently. "I'm already hungry. Let's not add aching head to the mix too. I'm not used to having a real body."

York glanced at the clock on her wall. "It's been three hours since they sent us up here. I haven't heard a peep. If this was a trick, I'm going to tear every one of them into tiny pieces. Then I'm gonna eat them all."

Morgan sat on the edge of her bed, fully dressed once more. She simply stared at her husband. "It will be fine. Right?"

He came to her quickly and bent before her, cupping her face in the process. "I love you, darlin'. I will not lose you. Understand?"

"I do," she returned. "And I love you. Can you sit down? All the pacing is making me nuts."

"Sorry, darlin'," he said softly. "I'm raring to go."

"I noticed."

There was a knock on the door a second before it blew inward in a dramatic fashion.

York threw himself over Morgan, protecting her from impact. When everything cleared, two men she didn't know were there, grinning in a lecherous manner. They had their hands out, and each had long dagger-like fingernails. They flashed fangs next.

Morgan froze.

"Oh good. The spell worked," said one of the men. "Get her!"

York spun around and stood tall, looking fine despite taking a door to the back only seconds prior. He snarled.

The men attempted to charge into her room but bounced off an unseen force. They struck the hallway wall with such vigor they left body indentations.

Morgan moved to her feet and gasped. Was that the spell her mother talked about? The warding?

One of the men was quicker than the other to get up and tried to gain access to her room again. It ended the same way.

York twisted to face her. "I'm going out there. You are to remain here. Am I clear?"

"Yes," she said.

He rushed out and into the excitement, tackling both men at once. Her husband was a force all unto himself, making short work of the enemy. When he was finished with them, he glanced into the room and put a hand out, running it back and forth at the threshold of the room. He grinned. "Heck of a warding. Momma would be envious of it even. Stay here, darlin'. I'm gonna see a man about a contract."

With that, he raced away, leaving her in her room, standing there, looking out at two very immobile Collective members. When she was convinced they were dead and gone and no longer a threat, Morgan eased closer to the doorway. She stood there, debating on leaving the safety of the room.

A giant explosion rocked the house, and then there was simply silence that followed.

Concerned for York and the others, Morgan sprinted from the room and into the hallway. The minute she cleared the doorway and the wards of her room, she heard chaos from the lower level. She understood then that the wards had blocked it all.

"Got ya!" shouted a man with a shaved head as he grabbed hold of her and yanked her backward.

He hadn't been there only moments prior.

"You're coming with me," he said, his hot breath skating over her cheek. "Your father wants a word with you."

Morgan elbowed him in the ribs, and the moment he lessened his hold on her, she broke free and ran for the stairs. Right before she reached the top of the stairs, the burning need to get down came over her, and she listened to her gut. She dropped to the floor, and the man stumbled over her back, falling down the long, long master staircase. It looked as if it hurt.

A lot.

When he came to rest at the base of the stairs, he didn't move.

Morgan hesitated momentarily before rushing down the stairs. She leaped over the man's body and then ran in the direction of her father's home office.

As she came around the corner, she found Spike and Booker engaged in battle with multiple Collective members in the center of the formal living room. Morgan's mother was fighting with three men at once.

For a second, all Morgan could do was stare in wonder at her mother, who had always seemed above getting a hair out of place. Now here Muffy was throwing a grown man through the air as if he weighed nothing. Muffy hissed at one of the men and defied gravity, going at him.

Two other men came from the other direction and charged Muffy.

Morgan reacted without thinking. She went at them and hit one head on. The impact rattled her to her core but did far worse to the other guy. He went flying backward as if he'd hit a concrete wall.

There wasn't time to think about it more.

Morgan ducked as the other man took a swing at her. She came up and punched him right in the gut, causing him to bend forward. When he did, she pushed him hard, and he toppled over the coffee table.

There was another massive boom, and she turned just in time to see a man come hurtling through the wall. He landed on the floor near Morgan's feet. She stared at the hole in the wall to find her mate on the other side, looking less than pleased. His gaze was locked on her.

"Darlin', I told you to stay in your room!" shouted York.

She opened her mouth to defend her actions, and York's body launched into the air. She knew it wasn't his doing. Everything in her shut off as she watched him flying upward. There was a faint buzzing around her that she ignored as she moved with a speed that stunned even her. She reached York in no time flat.

She put her hands in the air a second before the buzzing returned. It suddenly felt as though static energy was coursing through her veins. As she looked to the left, she saw her father there, his arms outstretched in York's direction. She knew he'd done something with magic to harm her mate, and that didn't work for her.

Not one bit.

Morgan let go of the feeling of static. Raw power shot forth from her. There was so much of it that it could be seen as clear as day. The power went right at her father and knocked him over onto the floor.

He came up snarling, his eyes narrow with anger. "You're supposed to be dead."

"Been there," she said with a shrug. "Done that."

His jaw tightened. "I see you inherited something from me after all. But you're new to using your magic. No real match for me."

"M-Morgan," said York, sounding pained. "Run!"

She didn't feel like running. She felt like knocking some sense into the man who'd created her. The man who should have been a true father to her. As her anger built, so did the knowledge that she came from his bloodline. If she dared to let herself take the path of hate, she'd be no better than him.

Instead, she squared her shoulders and stood tall. "I want the contract. Where is it?"

York grunted but pushed to his feet, looking slightly banged up as he did.

Her mother threw another man and came to stand near Morgan. "I got it and York has it now."

Just then, York reached into his back pocket and withdrew a piece of paper. "Here. I got down just in time to see she'd gotten it. Then from what I can gather, all hell broke loose."

Her father looked past her. "Muffy, you are weak! How could you side with them? You know what will happen to us if we don't honor the contract. We'll spend eternity locked in hell being tortured."

"It's what we deserve," said Muffy. She moved up beside Morgan and put her arm around her. "She's our daughter. Our baby girl. To bargain with her life and her soul was wrong, Barton."

"She is a means to an end," snapped Morgan's father.

Morgan took a calming breath and then shook her head. "I'd take offense that my father thinks that of me, but *he* doesn't. My father loves me."

That earned her a few questionable looks. Even the man who'd had a hand in her creation appeared baffled. Morgan cleared her throat. "Luc. He's been like a father to me ever since I can remember. And for thirty years, he's been that *and* my friend. My father is the devil, and yet he's still a better guy than you will ever be, Barton."

Millie walked up behind Barton slowly, making no sound as she did.

York lifted the contract higher and said something in Latin. She really wished she'd paid more attention when Luc had attempted to teach her the dead language.

Whatever he said made Barton flip out and begin to beg and shout for York to stop.

One second the contract was there, and the next, it was up in flames. It burned away to ash in seconds.

Muffy turned Morgan to face her. She hugged her. "I love you, and I'm sorry."

Morgan returned the embrace just as Millie slashed out at Barton with an insanely long arm. She caught the man by the scruff of the neck and flung him like a rag doll at the wall. He hit with a sickening thud and then fell to the floor, no longer moving.

Millie eased forward more. "He lives. I need to get him to a holding cell in hell. Luc will be expecting him now that the contract has been broken. Muffy."

Muffy nodded and released Morgan. "I know I have to go with you to serve my time."

"Wait," said Morgan quickly, grabbing her mother's hand. "No. It's over. You helped me. You protected me."

Millie sighed. "Child, she has to do her penance. She knew that from the start."

"Her penance?" asked Morgan, shaking her head as York came for her.

Millie glanced off to the right, looking at something Morgan couldn't see. "Don't worry, Morgan. Luc will go easy on her. I'm thinking she'll serve a term of about thirty

years in what we'd consider minimum security. Unlike Barton. He'll have eternity. Now,
you and your husband have something to do
before you head back to your time."

Muffy winked at Morgan. "I love you,
honey. Be safe, and I'll see you soon. I
promise."

Booker and Spike came closer as well.
They hugged her between them and then
stepped back.

"Take care, kid," said Spike. "I'll escort
your mom to hell and watch over her.
Okay?"

"T-thank you," managed Morgan,
tearing up.

Booker kissed the top of her head. "I will
get you and your mate to the concert. I'm
told you need to be there. And from there,
the coin in your pocket can get you both
home. Normally, between it and the brooch,
there would be enough magic to move one
of you, but since you're mated, it'll take you
both. Two-for-one kind of special."

Chapter Fourteen

PRESENT DAY

Morgan landed on the floor of the antiques shop, and York was close behind. He ended up on top of her, and she groaned. The man was hardly small. In fact, he felt a lot like a house had landed on her. Suddenly, Morgan was sympathetic to the witch from *The Wizard of Oz*.

"Ouch," she said in a hushed whisper.

"Sorry, darlin'." He rolled off her fast and ended up entangled in creepy dolls and wood body parts. He shot up fast and jumped to the side, doing the heebie-jeebies dance as if the dolls might get him. "Are they off me?"

She laughed. "Yes. You are safe from the childhood play items and fake body parts."

He stared down at her with wide eyes. "One of them was like a demon portal or something."

She stared at the blonde-haired, blue-eyed one next to her. "Was it this one? Seems the type."

He gave it a look that said he wasn't sure if it was a portal to something nasty or not.

"You took on the Collective and my father, but a doll scares you?" she questioned.

"I know where to place my fear," returned her husband.

They'd gotten to the concert, and even though York had wanted to save her from her fate, he'd let it happen, knowing if he dared stop her death, they might not end up a couple. He'd gone into the venue and spoken to the Morgan of the past, and he'd even killed four of the five assassins who had been sent to the concert for her on that night. She'd had to practically sit on him to keep him from ending the one who actually did kill her.

She hadn't been sure the coin and the brooch had enough power to get either of them back to the present. As much as she'd enjoyed the '80s, she did not want to be stuck there.

Morgan rolled onto her side to find Betty, Louis, Petey, and Luc all standing there, staring at her and York.

Louis had one hand on the phone receiver and Betty was near him, her hand on top of his. His jaw hung open. "You're back? You *just* left."

York helped her to her feet and slid an arm around her waist. "Just left? We've been gone nearly a full day."

Luc shook his head. "No. By our time, you've been gone about ten seconds."

"I'm never going to get used to this time thing," said York.

Betty grinned. "Dear, it gets better with practice. Then again, there are days I don't quite recall my name, so maybe you are onto something."

Morgan made a move to retrieve Betty's brooch from her skirt pocket only to discover it, along with the coin, was missing. She gasped. "Oh Betty! Your brooch! I lost it. I'm so sorry."

Betty took her hand from Louis's and moved slowly toward Morgan. She reached out and patted Morgan's cheek gently. "No worries. It's on its way back to me as we speak."

"It is?" asked Morgan, unsure how that was possible since it was more than likely lost back in the '80s. She bent and gave the older woman a hug. "Thank you for making sure I saw the truth about my mother."

Betty gave a curt nod and then stepped back, motioning to Luc as she did. "He's had a lot of secrets he's had to hold tight to for years now. Even removed himself from the equation to avoid learning something he shouldn't about your future."

Morgan met Luc's gaze and then ran to him, tossing her arms around his neck and hugging him tight.

He lifted her off her feet and held her for a moment.

She whispered to him, "Thank you for being the father that mine should have been."

He set her down and looked up, blinking a good deal.

"Uh, is the devil about to cry?" asked Louis, sounding shocked.

"He's a big softy," said Petey, as he withdrew a red handkerchief from his pocket and proceeded to blow his nose on it, tearing up as well. He held it out to Luc.

Luc declined with a wave of his hand.

Smart.

"Nobody cries alone in my presence," said Petey with a nod. "Made that a rule long ago. Speaking of rules, anyone else sensing something is different with York and Morgan? Are they mated?"

"W-what?" asked Louis, paling considerably. "Brother? You claimed her in ten seconds?"

Morgan laughed.

York sighed. "And they say you got the brains in the womb. And yes, I did claim her."

Petey's tears gave way to a huge smile that lit the man's face. He looked between Morgan and York. "By the power vested in me, I now pronounce you were-shark and ghost."

York was to her in a heartbeat, taking her hand in his and kissing her knuckles. "About that ghost thing."

Petey sniffed the air and then his eyes widened. "Great jumpin' jitterbugs! She's not a ghost anymore."

York increased his hold on her hand. "No. She's not one any longer."

Betty lifted her shoulders, the smallest of giggles coming from her. "Of course she's not. When I put a body back with its soul, it stays that way. Who do you think you're dealing with here? Some entry-level demon?"

"I have to hand it to you, Betty," said Luc, pride in his voice. "You've still got it."

"Never lost it," she corrected.

Just then, the door to the shop opened and Morgan glanced over to find her mother standing there, the light of the day at her back. Muffy's hair was longer now and it wasn't done in an '80s style. It looked current, and her mother barely looked to be in her thirties. She had on a cream-colored sweater that hung to her knees, brown leggings, and matching brown boots. A red scarf was around her neck.

"Mom?" asked Morgan. "What? How? You're out in the daylight?"

Muffy motioned to Luc. "He might have had a little something to do with it all."

"You're not trapped in hell?" asked Morgan, relief rushing through her as she went to her mother quickly and hugged her.

Muffy embraced her back. "No. I was on guard duty for your body for the duration it was there. When it vanished, I knew the time had come. I gathered some old friends and we headed this way."

With that, she stepped back, and Morgan saw Millie there behind her. Millie had a hedgehog in one arm and was holding what looked to be a cage with a blanket over it in the other.

"Millie!" exclaimed Morgan. "You're here! And you brought Spike."

"Oh, yay. Spike," said York, sounding anything but excited.

Muffy took Spike from Millie and handed him off to Luc. "Can you please lift the curse that keeps returning him to this form? He's sorry he beat you at chess."

Luc stared down at the hedgehog. "No he's not. He's thinking about how he's going to challenge me again the second he can."

"Luc," said Muffy with a stern note to her voice.

"Fine," returned Luc.

"Hey, let's not return him to human form right this second," said York, moving forward quickly. "I don't want to see his junk. If you catch my drift."

"I don't blame you," said Betty. "Human man-parts are not very impressive."

Millie nodded in agreement. "That's what I said."

Luc groaned. "Oh goodie. The Sisters Six are nearly complete once again. Can't wait to see what plagues they bring about."

"We can do that again?" asked Betty with nothing short of pure elation on her face.

"No," said Luc in a deep voice.

Millie and Betty both began to pout.

Louis hurried to Millie. "Hi. I'm Louis. Nice to meet you, Mildred. We've heard a lot about you from Betty. What do you have here?"

He eased the cage from her grasp and went to remove the cover.

Millie caught his wrist. "Hold on. Are your windows UV-treated for vampires?"

"They are," said Louis.

York groaned louder this time. "Wonderful. Mr. Haughty, I presume?"

Muffy laughed. "Yes. Booker is with us. His curse runs out today as well. He'll be a free man."

Morgan tensed. "You've all suffered another thirty years because of me?"

"No, honey," said Muffy. "We all willingly did what needed to be done to make sure you were safe and sound. We love you. It's what family does for one another."

Morgan couldn't stop the tears from coming.

Petey thrust his handkerchief out to her.

She nearly took it without paying attention, but York intervened. "Darlin', no fussing over this. They're right. Family does this for each other."

Morgan tried to stop tearing up but

couldn't. "I don't know why I can't stop crying."

Millie laughed. "Sweetie, pregnancy hormones will do it to you. I can't wait for the little ones to get here."

"I'm sorry, what?" asked Morgan, emotionally sobering instantly at the mention of pregnancy hormones.

Millie glanced at her sister.

Betty nodded. "It's true. The girls will be here before you know it. I can't wait. They look like their mother but act like their father."

Morgan grabbed for York's hand only to find it wasn't where she'd last thought it was. Turning, she expected to find him right behind her.

While he technically was behind her, he wasn't standing.

He was flat on his back, lying on the dolls he was so afraid of.

Louis rushed over to his brother and bent. He checked him over. "He fainted."

Petey nodded and rubbed his chin. "Doll fright. I get it. Scare the dickens out of me too."

"Someone should get him off the floor," said Luc.

Morgan snorted. "Not before I call his sisters, his mother, and his grandmother to come over and take a bunch of pictures. I'm going to need your phone."

Luc tossed it to her, and she went to work capturing the moment.

"My husband," she said, emotions welling in her. "The *alpha*."

THE END

About the Author

Dear Reader

Did you enjoy this title and want to know more about Mandy M. Roth, her pen names and all the titles she has available for purchase (over 100)?

About Mandy:

New York Times & *USA TODAY* Bestselling Author Mandy M. Roth loves 80s music and movies and wishes leg warmers would come back into fashion. She also thinks the movie The Breakfast Club should be mandatory viewing for...okay, everyone. When she's not dancing around her office to the sounds of the 80s or writing books, she can be found designing book covers for New York publishers, small presses, and indie authors.

Learn More:

To learn more about Mandy and her

pen names, please visit www.Mandy-Roth.com

For latest news about Mandy's newest releases and sales subscribe to her newsletter: Sign Up For Mandy's Newsletter

Want to see all Mandy's books? Click here.

Printable PDF list of all Mandy's titles: Click here.

To join Mandy's Facebook Reader Group: The Roth Heads.

Review this title:

Please consider leaving an honest review on the vendor site in which you purchased this title. Reviews help to spread the word and boost overall sales. This means more books in the series you love.

Thank you!

facebook.com/AuthorMandyRoth

twitter.com/mandymroth

instagram.com/mandymroth

goodreads.com/mandymroth

pinterest.com/mandymroth

bookbub.com/authors/mandy-m-roth

youtube.com/mandyroth

amazon.com/author/mandyroth

CPSIA information can be obtained
at www.ICGtesting.com
Printed in the USA
LVHW031045181119
637664LV00001B/212/P